COMING HOME

KAY HALL BECKMAN

Happy Reading

Kay Hall Beckman

PublishAmerica
Baltimore

Softcover 9781627723749
PUBLISHED BY PUBLISHAMERICA, LLLP
www.publishamerica.com
Baltimore

Printed in the United States of America

ACKNOWLEDGEMENTS:

To My Great-Granddaughter
Faelynn Spilker
You are the sunshine to my soul.

CHAPTER 1

Faelynn sat on the plane with her briefcase sitting on her lap, half opened. Since she would be on the plane for most of the day, she had intended on working during the flight. She could catch up on some paperwork, she had been neglecting. She looked around at the activity of the other passengers then decided to wait on her work until the plane had taken off and was in the air, hoping the noise would settle down somewhat.

She stared out the window watching the clouds go by as her mind drifted back to when she got the call from Dr. Wellington, explaining that her grandmother was seriously ill and not expected to live. It had been quite a shock to hear that because her grandmother had never said anything in her letters about being sick.

Of course, their letters were polite letters not the loving and gentle letters of a grandmother who had loved her granddaughter. Faelynn had looked like her mother with blond hair and blue eyes. She did not inherit the dark coloring of her father nor his dark hair.

Her grandmother, Laura had never loved her. She had felt more like a duty, her grandmother had to endure. Faelynn sighed, *she shouldn't feel that way about her only living relative but she did.* Yet, she wondered, why her grandmother hadn't told her of her sickness in one of her few letters.

Her thoughts drifted back to the town she was coming back too. Where she grew up but left as quickly as possible. She had been dreading this day for many years because she didn't want to come back, her past held nothing for her. She didn't want to have to deal with the problems she left behind. She especially didn't want to have to take care of her grandmother's affairs because it would be too painful to have to be there again.

While growing up she thought she would live there all her life. Her parents Jack and Caroline Myers were both born there and her grandmother Laura and grandfather Earl had lived there for as long as she could remember. Grandfather Earl had passed away when she was a young child of four. She was an only child and her parents had left her with her grandmother to take a second honeymoon to Europe.

Their plane crashed over the Atlantic and no survivors were ever found. She was devastated at the loss of the only people that loved her. They doted on her, giving her all of their love. She remembered her mother helping her learn to read or her father teaching her how to tie her shoes or how to ride her bicycle. Her security was lost that day and she never felt it again at her grandmother's home.

Her grandmother really didn't want the responsibility of raising a child. But there was nowhere else for her to go, except to put her in an orphanage. She was sure her grandmother would have done that except the town would have gossiped about her, making her rethink the thought. She was all but ignored growing up and was left to the nanny to raise her properly and to make sure she attended school and learned her social manners.

It is strange how some things happen that could rearrange your life forever. She had gone to Crandall Elementary and then to Union High School, where she graduated. She drew the attention of Richard Helms, whom she thought to be the best looking guy in school. He would look at her when he passed her in the halls and smile. She would almost swoon as her heart fluttered about in her chest. They had started hanging out together when he sat down at her table during a lunch period and they had talked the entire time. They seemed to drift from one subject to another without noticing. He was easy to talk to and they enjoyed each other's company.

They had even gone to the movies and dances together at times. He would stop by her locker just to say hello or she would pass him in the hall and say *hello*. They had shared their first tender kiss at a movie theater after watching a beautiful love story.

They didn't date exclusive because her grandmother would never hear of that. She was sure, so they remained friends throughout school. Both She and Richard had plans to attend college. So a long-term relationship was out of the question. Careers came first for both of them. There were many girls at school that had hoped to catch his eye for that all-important invitation to the prom. She felt very special when she received his invitation and quickly accepted. She couldn't help but smile for the next few days until the day of the prom drew near. He arrived at the appointed time with an exquisite corsage for her simple blue organdy dress.

They had even stolen a kiss under the dogwood tree outside her home on their way to his car. He was the football team captain. He was over six feet with dark brown hair and blue eyes and was very handsome, with broad shoulders and long legs. He could have had any girl in the school. She was surprised and pleased that he had chosen her to ask to the prom. They had danced the night away gazing into each other's eyes. It felt so right between them that night. Richard was very attentive the entire night and seemed to be truly hers because he never danced with anyone else. He had hardly left her side except to get them refreshments. It had been a perfect night until they had started their return trip to her home. It was then that she discovered he had ulterior motives for the ending of their night. He pulled off the road into a place that was known for lovers who wanted to make out, as they say. He stopped his car in a secluded place between two large trees where it couldn't be seen from the road. It was almost as if he had been there plenty of times before. She was confused because he had never brought her here before tonight.

Her eyes blazed at him, "I hope you're not planning on stopping here because I'm not that kind of girl. I thought you knew that. I'm not interested in having a backseat relationship and I'm not going to start one now." He shut the engine off and reached for her, pulling her close to him for a kiss. She jerked back and slid to the opposite door. He tried to persuade her to come back into his arms but she fought him off. He sighed as he raked his hand through his hair, "Faelynn, you mean a lot to me. I wanted to stop here so we could have a chance to talk. I have a lot of feelings for you and thought you shared those feelings." He tried to pull her back into his arms to kiss her. She reached for the door handle and opened it. He angrily shouted, "Stop?" But she didn't. "I've explained to you that I'm not the kind of person you take to a place like this, thinking you're going to get me to do something I'm not going to do. I want to be taken home immediately." He turned the key to spark the engine and squealed the tires getting back to the main road. He dropped her off without as much as a good night or an apology. It had spoiled what had been a very nice night. She rushed to her room and flung his flowers into the trash. She quickly undressed and went to bed. The dam of un-shed tears burst and flowed easily. Her dreams had been shattered and her innocence of youth forever damaged. She would never trust another man as she had trusted him.

He did call her the next day, "Can we meet somewhere and talk? I owe you an apology, please Faelynn?" She held the phone for a minute staring at the wall behind her before answering him, "I don't think it's a good idea Richard. I think last night pretty much summed up our relationship, don't you? I think it would be best if we just left things as they are. Please don't call me again." He tried to speak before she hung up the phone, to plead with her one last time but was too late, it went dead. He hung up the phone reluctantly with no other options left to him. He whispered, "I did respect you Faelynn, I love you." She was still upset at the way he had tried to treat her and decided she wanted nothing to do with him or his attitude. He had burst her idea that he was a perfect person, now she knew he wasn't.

In the next few weeks Richard worked hard and put in long hours for his father and made his plans to attend college in another state. It was just as well because he knew Faelynn would probably never speak to him again. He just couldn't figure out where it all went wrong and why she wouldn't at least let him apologize and explain what he had intended. He stuffed her gift into the bottom of his chest closing the top and locking it away.

Faelynn attended Covington College because there was no money for the big universities. After High School she started her classes at the beginning of summer so she could get a jump-start on her college credits. It helped her to forget him for a while but in her room at night as she studied, she thought of him and wondered how a young budding romance could have gone so wrong. She threw herself into her studies so that she could finish early and move out of town as fast as possible. She had finished college at the top of her class, and a year early with her degree in Business Management and Advertising; she was ready to move into the workforce.

She had searched for jobs at the other end of the world as far as she was concerned, so that she didn't have to be reminded of this town, her grandmother or Richard Helms. Even after the years of college she still missed him. There seemed to be no one that could take his place. The few times she dated only lasted only a short while. She lost interest in the man eventually and stopped seeing them. When they would call for another date she would make excuses not to go out with them anymore. She often wondered if her life would ever be pain free of Richard or if he would remain with her forever. She hoped the change of scenery would help her heal.

Her grandmother had set up a trust fund that was the insurance from her parent's death. She didn't want to use it but did when it was needed to finish college and get herself set up in a city far from Covington, Ga. She had found a job in Portland, Oregon with an advertising firm called Webb Marketing Incorporated. They were a very smart firm that was established for many years with a long list of loyal customers.

Faelynn had worked her way up from the entry level to a manager level within a few years. She enjoyed her job and got a lot of personal achievement and satisfaction from it. She had even dated a few times but many of the dates were business acquaintance. So they really didn't count.

She dated one of her co-workers named Michael Shane for almost a year. His father owned a large construction company that Michael had worked at during his school years. His dad had hoped Michael would come back and take over some of the business for him but Michael's career ideas were set. He liked the fast paced job in advertising and its many perks. He was quite handsome with jet-black hair and dark eyes; he was over six feet tall with an athlete's build. She suspected that he was about to give her an engagement ring before she was called back home. She wasn't sure she wanted it because she wasn't ready to get married. Their relationship was more like friends than lovers. There was no hot sparks or burning desire between them, just mutual respect for each other. It had been a relief to get away from the office for a while to give her time to think about their relationship.

She had made friends with several other single women who went out to dinner occasionally together. Mostly to keep up with what is going on with each of them. They went to a local club to see a new band play or just to see what was going on. None of them were into the pick-up scene so they didn't stay long enough for it to become a problem.

Her grandmother crept back into her thoughts pushing all thought of Michael and her life in Oregon away. As her grandmother aged, she had invited her back to her home for many holidays but Faelynn always had something to do or work to catch up on. She did go back and visit once when her grandmother had fallen ill with a virus and stayed a week until she had re-cooperated and was ready to resume her normal life.

Her grandmother had asked if she would like to move back east to be closer to her but Faelynn couldn't imagine why. She could hardly wait to leave again. She had tried to keep a conversation going with her grandmother but it was hard since they barely knew each other and the two reasons they did have in common died a long time ago.

She knew that her grandmother belonged to the country club and attended the community church, often entertaining a group of ladies on a regular basis for some charity she supported. She also belonged to several other community organizations, which she seemed to cater too. That is how she spent most of her time going to this meeting or that meeting. She kept an active social calendar that kept her quite busy.

Faelynn had a lot of time to think on this long trip back to Georgia, perhaps she might even solve the world's problems before she got there. She smiled at that thought. It did seem to be a good time to reflect over her life and see if the choices she had made were good ones. She loved the Oregon coastline with the white beaches and spent her vacations there. There was so much to see and do in Oregon; it had become her home replacing the one she had lived at in Georgia. She spent a lot of weekends driving up and down the coast looking at the sea or stopping for lunch in some out of the way place. She would stop to buy some quick snacks and drinks to have a picnic on a deserted beach, watching the waves come in and splash against the rocks.

She visited the museums and local events that were taking place during her visit. She went to the big farmer's market to find her fresh vegetables and the flea market to pick up a bargain now and again. Sometimes in the spring they would have an outdoor art show where new or young artist came to sell their wares. It was always a big hit and brought the crowds to see what the new art was going to be. She had even bought a piece or two for her apartment.

Michael and her would rent a boat and go out into the deeper water to fish or just to swim some. It was peaceful spending the day lying on the deck as the water splashed against the boat. Michael was very courteous and kind to her when he escorted her around town. He never took things for granted and always asked her out several days in advance to give her time to be ready. He never called spontaneously to ask her to go somewhere with him. She always wondered *why?* But it didn't matter she enjoyed the time she spent with him. They were both quiet people and enjoyed spending time together or alone. There wasn't a lot of hugging and kissing because Faelynn hadn't been raised that way.

She was brought out of her dream state by the revving of the airplane's engine on the descent onto the Atlanta Airport runway. She was here. *Where had the time gone? She meant to get some work done but hadn't?*

No one would be there at the airport to meet her because no one knew she would be coming. After retrieving her bags she made her way out to the sidewalk so she could hail a cab. She finally got a cab and gave him her grandmother's address. She was whisked away in a long line of other taxis headed in different directions.

He stopped at her grandmother's home and carried her luggage into the living room where she gave him a tip for his help. He closed the door and left the curb within minutes. She looked around the room and it looked as if nothing had been moved or changed since she had been here last.

She took her bags up to her room to freshen up before going to the hospital to see how her grandmother was doing. When she opened the door to the room and put her luggage on the bed as she looked around her old room. It looked the same. She wondered why her grandmother hadn't redecorated it after all these years.

She stepped into the shower and the water felt refreshing on her skin after that long airplane ride. She was drying her hair when the phone rang. She picked it up, "Hello." The voice on the other end belonged to Michael. She didn't want to stay on the phone long because she wanted to get to the hospital for visiting hours, "Michael was there something I forgot to tell you about my work? I have just arrived and am on my way to the hospital now." There was a pause and the answer came. "I just called to make sure you made it there safe and sound. I did want to talk to you for a minute but it can wait until tomorrow. Have a nice visit with your grandmother and I hope she gets along good and gets to feeling better. Now that her granddaughter is back with her, it will please her I'm sure."

Faelynn felt obligated to say, "Thank you for your well wishes but I don't know the situation, so I'm not sure what is going on with her yet. We'll talk tomorrow and then I'll have more news." They said their goodbye and she dressed to go to the hospital.

She drove her grandmother's car to Covington General Hospital just as the visiting hours had started. It was only about two miles or so from their home. She stopped by the nurse's station, "What room is Laura Myers in and who is the doctor handling her case?" The nurse advised her, "She is on the fourth floor and Doctor Wellington has her case file." Faelynn went to the elevator to reach the floor and her room was across from it. She stepped into the room to see an elderly woman lying on the bed. She had gray hair and looked so fragile. *This couldn't be her grandmother. She didn't look like that. She was too active to look so old.*

Out of the corner of her eye she saw a doctor washing his hands in the sink in the small bathroom adjoining the room. He turned to look at her and smiled. He held out his hand, "I'm Doctor Wellington and you must be Faelynn." He took her hand in his and he kept it there while he spoke. "Your grandmother has had a series of problems that have occurred recently and had to be admitted to the hospital." He looked at his patient who was now sleeping, "Can we go downstairs to the cafeteria to have a cup of coffee?" Faelynn nodded her head as he took her elbow and ushered her back into the elevator to the first floor.

He brought two cups of coffee to the table and sat down next to her. Faelynn was impatient to know what the problem was so she inquired first, "What seems to have happened to my grandmother? She doesn't look like the same woman I left here a few years back. When did her health start failing?" The doctor sipped his coffee as he waited for her to finish speaking. He looked at her face seeing the concern, "Just how long ago did you leave our town?" Faelynn stopped drinking and stared at him as she mentally figured out how long she had been gone. "I guess I have been gone a while, almost six years or more."

The doctor shook his head wondering why her granddaughter had stayed away, "It seems that she first had a mild stroke about four years ago and since that time she had a heart attack two years ago. We put a stint in two arteries then. She did pretty well until she fell down her steps and cracked her left hipbone. She had to have a replacement and since then it hasn't been easy for her. She is very strong willed and independent and won't let anyone help her. She wouldn't even let me call you when she needed someone with her. She told me that you had your own life to live and you didn't need to come back to take care of an old woman, who hadn't taken care of you, when you needed her."

An icy hand gripped Faelynn's heart. Her grandmother had needed her and she wasn't there for her. She shivered to think about how lonely her grandmother had been while she refused to return here to live. But she didn't feel she was wanted here. She didn't feel that this was her home, not one she could return to and live.

The doctor brought her back to the present, "It seems that she has gone into a deep depression and no longer wants to live. The only reason I broke my promise to her and called you is that she is now refusing to eat or drink. Normally, in her condition it would take little more than a week or so for her to die. I felt you had a right to know what was going on with her and to see her for yourself. Perhaps, she will respond to you, since you're here." He looked down into his now cold cup of coffee, picking it up as he whispered, "And I certainly hope she does."

He sat his coffee back down and looked at her for a long moment, "Please, go up to see your grandmother and see if she will allow you to persuade her to eat again. Perhaps your presence will encourage her to do so." He stood and left the table. She sat there in a trance. Why would her grandmother choose to die like this? She was an active person with plenty of friends to keep her busy.

She stood and put her cup in the trash bin and on wooden legs walked again to the elevators to the fourth floor. She eased open the door and stood watching her grandmother sleep. She seemed so different, much older and more fragile. She walked silently over to the chair that sat beside her bed and sat down. She looked at the woman in the bed, she seemed darker, her skin rough and her eyes sunk back into her face. Surely this wasn't her grandmother but all the features were the same. She had the thin drawn lips, the stubborn jaw and with the same nose as her father's.

What had happened to make her give up living? She was so happy here in her own home and with her friends. She never had time for her only granddaughter, but all the time in the world for her friends. Where were her friends now? They should be here filling this room, encouraging her to eat and go on living. Why weren't they here? She looked around the room not one flower was there. Didn't her friends know she was here?

Faelynn couldn't help but feel sorry for the time that had been lost between grandmother and granddaughter. She hurt because there had been no love between them. They had shared a house but not their lives. Her grandmother had made it very clear to her that she was intruding on her life. What was she expected to do now? She didn't make their life this way. How was she supposed to change it now?

She had sat there so deep in her own thought she didn't see her grandmother open her eyes. She lay there looking at the young woman sitting beside her bed. She hardly recognized Faelynn. She had grown up and was a very beautiful young lady who had a life of her own. What was she doing here? She reached out to touch her granddaughter who seemed to be looking out the window behind her without seeing anything.

Faelynn jumped when her hand had been touched. She looked down to see her grandmother looking at her. She hardly recognized her even now that she knew it was her grandmother. Faelynn reached out to hold her hand, "Grandmother, I heard you had been very ill. How are you feeling? Is there anything I can do for you?"

Her grandmother held her hand; it was the first physical contact they had experienced in years. If only she could go back and change all those years, but it was too late now. She was surprised to see her granddaughter sitting in her room, "How did you learn that I was in the hospital?" Faelynn looked at her as she thought *should she tell on the doctor and probably get him in trouble for doing what he thought was best*? No, she would lie. "I had to come to Atlanta on business and I stopped by to visit with you for a few days." She wasn't sure her grandmother bought her story but she didn't challenge it.

"What happened that caused you to be in the hospital? Was one of your friends with you when you became ill?" Faelynn watched as her grandmother thought on her questions. It didn't take much to realize that her friends hadn't been around much since she had fallen sick. "Grandmother, how long have you been this sick? Why didn't you call me? I would have come out to take care of you."

Her grandmother looked at her face for some time before answering her question. "I didn't call you because there is nothing you can do for me. I am old, my health is bad and in the end we die. I suspect that won't be too far off." Faelynn was alarmed at her cavalier attitude about dying. She had been so vibrant in her life just to give up and ready to die.

CHAPTER 2

The elevator doors opened and she stepped into the lobby of the hospital. She was not looking at anyone, just walking with her head bent in thought. She heard her name being called and looked up to see her grandmother's doctor. She stopped and waited for him to reach her.

He took her arm and walked on toward the front doors of the hospital. He turned to her and inquired how their meeting had went, "How did it go with your grandmother? Did she respond to you?" Faelynn slowed her walking as she tried to answer his question; "She did speak to me but I fear that my being here is not going to change anything with her. She seems cavalier about dying and was surprised to find me sitting by her bed.

I told her I was in Atlanta on a business trip and stopped by to visit with her but I don't think she bought it." She sighed, "I don't know what to do for her. We weren't close when I was dumped on her doorstep and when my parents died in an airplane crash and I had to live with her. I think she resented having to take care of me. I don't know what to tell you but I'm not sure that she wants me here at all."

The doctor seemed to be in thought also. He commented, "Will you come back to visit with her everyday to at least give her an opportunity to get to know you some?" Faelynn nodded her head *Yes,* but she still had her doubts that it would make any difference to her grandmother. He opened her door and when she got into the car, he closed the door, "Let's give it a little while, how long can you stay?" Faelynn looked at him before saying, "I guess I can stay as long as she needs me." He gave her a big smile and patted her car door; "Good, I'll see you tomorrow then."

She stopped at the local grocery store to get some food for a few days and a bottle of wine for later that night. She noticed how much larger the store had gotten from when she had lived there. She even saw a girl she had went to school with. Her name was Charlene Adams from her tenth grade history class. She was cashier at the store. They chatted a few minutes while she was checking out her groceries. Charlene inquired as to her visit, "So, how long are you in town for this visit?" Faelynn laughed and set more of her groceries on the belt, "I'm not sure, my grandmother is ill, so I am staying at her place until the doctor releases her. But when that will be, no one seems to know, at the moment."

She didn't want to make any commitments to do anything just yet until she found out what was going on with her grandmother. Charlene spoke again, "Well, if you get a free evening give me a call and we'll take in a movie or stop at the bar to see who all shows up." Faelynn agreed. "Perhaps, Grandmother will get well, and then we can do that." She picked up her few bags and left.

She went into the house and put her few groceries in the refrigerator. She climbed the stairs to change into some shorts and a top then came back down the stairs to the kitchen, where she could look out over the back yard. She stepped out onto the deck to see it was in bad need of cleaning up and some grass needed cutting. She needed to find someone to clean up the fallen limbs and twigs from the trees and move the brush that seemed to be clumped at several places.

She started down the steps but caught the railing just before the step gave way. She climbed back onto the deck and looked the steps over. They had been broken before and were rotted out and should be fixed right away. She walked back inside to get a pencil and pad so she could make some notes for the repairman. She thought; *it's possible her grandmother had fallen on the back steps the day she broke her hip.*

She stopped in the kitchen and put her chicken breast in the oven to bake along with a small potato. She could make her salad when she came back downstairs. She climbed the stairs to the upper rooms and looked into each one of them. She opened the door to her grandmother's room and looked around. It looked the same as it had when she left six years ago. Nothing in the room had changed, not even the long green drapes that had hung on the antique rods above the long windows.

She walked into the guest room, which no one had ever used and stood looking at the same thing that she had seen years ago. Why had her grandmother not at least changed the curtains for new ones? Surely, she had the money to redecorate. She would have to ask her about that and talk to her about some of her affairs.

She walked back down stairs to finish making dinner. Her salad was made and the potato buttered and the chicken breast had been sliced to perfection. She poured a nice cold glass of tea and sat at the kitchen table to eat her evening meal. She made notes on her pad of things to check on about the house.

After her meal, she washed up her dishes and left them on the drain board. She walked into the living room to see much of the furniture covered with sheets. She was surprised at all the changes she found in the house or the no changes she saw. How long had her grandmother let things go? What had happened to her friends that she cared so much about when she had lived in the house? She walked over to the desk and looked in the drawers for the phone book that was usually there. The more she looked around the more questions she had that needed answers.

She opened the book from page to page and she found many of the names marked through. Had they died? Placing the book back in the drawer she walked to the front door and stepped outside. There was a small wicker table with two chairs near the end of the long wraparound porch. She walked over to it and sat down. She watched the street as people and cars passed the house.

She began to relax as she noticed that the bush on the corner of the house, with large purple flowers had a nice fragrance that seemed to drift into the air. She looked at all the flowers that were planted near the house and wondered who had been taking care of them. There was a big white butterball bush on the other end of the porch that was also in bloom. It gave the house a warm, friendly; welcoming look even though she knew there was no warm friendly welcome waiting inside.

How different life could have been if her grandmother had loved her. They could have lived here together, happy and content to stay in this town for all her life. But it was much too late now. Too much time had passed and she had her own life and career to think of now.

Tomorrow, she would look for a repairman to do some work around the house and a gardener to do some work in the yard. At least it would look lived in again.

It was beginning to get dark so she went back into the house and cut on some lights and the television so she could watch the evening news. While she was sitting there she thumbed through the phone book looking for some numbers she could call tomorrow.

She got up to check the outside lights and to lock the doors. She noticed that the back porch light did not work another thing for the repairman to fix. The front porch light worked fine so she left it on for a while. The phone rang and she walked over to answer it. It was Mrs. Jones across the street, wondering who was at the house because she knew that her grandmother was in the hospital. Faelynn assured her that she would be there for a few weeks so not to worry that someone had broken into the house.

In the kitchen she poured herself a glass of wine and went back into the living room to watch a special report that was on the ten o'clock news. They were telling about the wild fires in California and southern Oregon burning the homes and destroying precious forestlands. She hated to see the fires destroy so much property. The smoke that hung over the area causing polluted air made it hard for everyone to breathe.

After cutting off the television she walked into the kitchen and rinsed her glass in the sink, putting it with the dishes to drain. She walked up the stairs after cutting off the downstairs lights. She opened the door to her room and stood at the window looking out at the street below her. It was quiet with only a few cars traveling on it now. Once in a while she saw a walker go by the house.

She guessed nothing had changed that through the years. Her grandmother still had good neighbors, which she was glad to know. She stretched and yawned crawling into her bed for a good night's sleep. She heard bells somewhere in the room but could not tell exactly where. She could not get awake enough to tell what it was or where it was happening.

With a jolt she sat straight up, she remembered, it was the phone. She dragged herself over to the table and answered it.

She sat down in the chair beside the table waiting for someone to answer. She spoke again into the phone, "Hello, Hello, is anyone there?" No one answered. She looked at the phone with a frown before replacing it back on its cradle. Who could be calling her at this hour and then not say anything?

Looking at the clock she discovered that it was six o'clock in the morning. Who would be calling this early anyway? Surely if it was the hospital they would have spoke to her. Perhaps it was Michael, but he would have spoke to her. Well, it must have been a bad connection and they will call back in a few minutes. She would just have to wait to see who it was.

She dressed and walked downstairs to get her breakfast as long as she was up anyway. She got the coffee perking and her toast in the toaster. That was her breakfast and it was plenty after her dinner last night she was still stuffed.

She walked back to the living room and cut off the outside light on the porch. She peeked up and down the street to see if anyone was walking this early. She did see a jogger or two with a dog running the street.

Faelynn had her work cut out for her today and she needed an early start too. She wanted the repairman and the yard work done today. The yard needs to be cut and the fallen leaves need raking. She took the phone book to the kitchen so she could call from there.

After her third cup of coffee and finishing off her toast she dialed a lawn business to see if she could get it done today. She hoped she had found a reliable service, she didn't remember this company when she lived here, a man answered the phone "Wheeler Lawn Service," "I'm looking for someone to do some yard work. Do you have someone available that can do it today?" The man on the other end of the phone inquired, "Where is the yard located and who will be paying for the service?"

Faelynn thought perhaps she might get it done today after all. She gave the address, "I am at 3429 Walnut Street and I am Faelynn Myers and I will be here until one o'clock if you could send them over this morning I could show them what needs to be done." He agreed to send someone over, "They will be there by eight o'clock to check in with you and then if you have to leave they can still get the yard done, well most of it done today. I have two other jobs for today also so it might be late when they're done."

Faelynn thought for a minute thumping her pencil against her cheek, "Okay, could you please tell me the name of the person that will be coming by?" The man spoke with pride about his employee, "Oh sure, his name will be David Stahl. He is a very trustworthy kid and has been working for me for several summers."

Faelynn felt relief knowing that the young man who came there would be a steady worker. She then asked one more question, "What is going to be the charge for the cleanup?" He knew he had to see the size of the yard before giving her a price, "I'll come by early this morning to see the yard and give you a price then. She replied, "Thank you Mr. Wheeler, I appreciate your getting to it so quickly."

She hung up the phone satisfied that some of the problems will be dealt with that day. Now for the repairman, she turned the page to where she had marked for the carpenter. She dialed the number and a man answered, "Jefferson Carpentry." She at least dialed the right number, "Hello, My name is Faelynn Myers and I live at 3429 Walnut Street and I need a few repairs done to the back porch and wondered if you might have someone that can stop by and give me a price on the job?"

The man hesitated then replied, "I can stop by there about ten this morning if someone is going to be there." Faelynn couldn't believe her luck. Wow, getting two jobs done in one day. "Yes, I'll be here and I appreciate your coming so soon. I'm sorry I didn't catch your name." There was another hesitation, "I'm sorry, my name is Steven Smith and I'll see you at ten then." Faelynn hung up the phone but wasn't very comfortable with the last call. She had this uneasy feeling for some reason. Perhaps she should call and cancel it. Then she chided herself by saying, *what's the matter with you, silly. No one will bother you here. It's a safe place to live.*

With her thought forgotten she picked up the house and made her bed, collecting the few things that needed to be washed put in the laundry basket to take to the laundry room. Time flew by faster than she had expected because she saw a young man walking to her front door.

She opened the door and greeted the young man before he had a chance to knock. She introduced herself and walked him to the back yard to see it. A few minutes later Mr. Wheeler arrived and joined them there. He looked around the yard and asked Faelynn, "What did you want David to do in the yard, other than cutting the grass and picking up the debris?" Faelynn replied with her ideas, "I would like to see it manicured and the weeds pulled from the flower beds and the trees trimmed. It looks a little ragged right now but it does clean up nicely."

Mr. Wheeler quoted her a price, which seemed very reasonable so she told him to go ahead and start working on it. Mr. Wheeler turned to his employee and stated, "David, go ahead and clean as much as you can and I'll drop around this afternoon and help you finish up. I have to go over to the

Wilcox's and finish trimming there too." David nodded and went to retrieve his tools from Mr. Wheeler's truck.

Faelynn looked at Mr. Wheeler, an aging man of late fifties with salt and pepper hair, "Thank you so much for getting right on this. My grandmother is in the hospital and it seems that she didn't have anyone looking after the yard." Mr. Wheeler looked at her for a minute before saying, "Yeah, I passed by here and wondered who lived here. I hadn't seen anyone taking care of the place and wondered what was going on. I was going to stop but with being so busy this time of year I hadn't had the chance."

She explained to him that she was just here visiting from Oregon where she lived and worked and would be staying here until her grandmother got better. She looked at her watch and sighed, "My goodness, it's time for the repairman to stop by so he can quote me a price for fixing the steps. They're in bad shape too." He watched her walk back to the house before climbing back into his truck to leave. He saw David working in the back yard mowing the grass as he turned the corner onto Oak Street. He saw a blue pickup stopping at the curb to her house.

He wondered how long she had been gone from here because he would have remembered seeing her around town if she had stayed here. He knew a lot of people in his business and worked for most of them. Traffic picked up so that was the last thought of the pretty young lady living on Walnut Street.

Faelynn met the man in the blue truck as she walked to the front of the house. She held out her hand and introduced herself to Steven Smith. "I have some back steps that are in need of some repair. If you will follow me I'll show you where they are." She noticed that Steven Smith was not a large man but short and stocky. He had black hair and eyes. He looked of Italian or Spanish descent. He was clean cut and seemed to have good manners. She showed him the broken and rotting steps, "I am not sure what else needs repair but I will keep your card in case I find something else." He looked her up and down then smiled, "The steps do look pretty dangerous and should be replaced quickly. I'll work up an estimate on it and drop it by later tonight. I have two other jobs ahead of you so it should not be more than a day or two before I can get it done." She was disappointed at that news because they needed to be fixed right away, "Thank you, Mr. Smith, I do appreciate your time and the quicker these are fixed the better I will feel about my grandmother using them."

She walked him back toward his truck and she went into the house to get ready to go to the hospital to visit her grandmother. Within a few minutes she was pulling out of her driveway en-route to the hospital. She didn't know why but she still felt a little twinge of apprehension about Steven Smith. What was it about him that made her leery?

The ride to the hospital didn't take but a few minutes and she pulled into a parking spot. Closing her door she looked around the hospital at how much it had grown and added on new wings since she had lived here. As she walked down the sidewalk toward the revolving door she felt someone behind her. She slowed down hoping they would pass her but they didn't. The person stepped up beside her and asked in that rich deep baritone voice; "Good afternoon, Faelynn, how are you today?" she looked up in surprise that someone would know her name. She smiled as she saw the handsome Dr. Wellington. "I'm fine, just getting used to being back here and catching up on some work I brought with me." He watched her expression then smiled, "I think your grandmother is improving a little.

She is still insisting she wants to die but perhaps you might turn that thinking around."

Faelynn studied a bit before saying; "I hope so because she was such a vibrant lady when I was growing up. She was always doing this or that to keep busy. I don't understand where all the friends she had back then have gone to. There is no one in her phone book anymore. Do you know what happened to stop them from coming to see her?" Dr. Wellington took her arm and guided her to a bench in a small garden of flowers, "Let's sit outside for a few minutes to talk."

She followed him to a cement bench back from the main walking area for privacy. He cleared his throat as he started to speak, "I'm not exactly sure what the whole thing was about but it seems that she had a disagreement with one of the older ladies and it seems that most of the group sided with the other woman. You know how it is in a small town when two ladies square off and most of the friend's side with one or the other. It makes for bad feelings all around. Your aunt was considered an outcast to the group after that.

What it was about, I'm not sure. Perhaps you might speak with one of them to know for sure. I know it made her sad and she lost the will to keep up her social life because of it. Please remember, I'm speaking to you in a private manner and as a friend. I don't want your grandmother to think I'm meddling into her personal life." Faelynn watched as something flickered across his face, a kind of sadness. "Thank you doctor, I won't breathe a word but it might help me to understand what she is going through. She might not want to live if she has lost all her friends over some squabble between them. I'll call one that I know is close to her to see if I can get the story from them."

They both stood and walked inside the hospital lobby. He bid her a good day and she walked into the elevator for the fourth floor. She stood outside her grandmother's room and watched the activity up and down the hall. Very few people came close to her room and only one nurse went inside to administer medicines.

What had the argument been about that caused her to lose all her friends? She couldn't imagine what subject so fiercely argued could cause a riff between all the ladies. They had been friends for years, attended social events together, played cards together. She could not even begin to imagine what source of contention could have done so much damage.

She walked into the room where the frail woman slept. She took her seat beside the bed and waited for her to wake. She watched out the window as people passed by walking into the hospital. She knew none of them, occasionally one would seem familiar but then it had to be someone from her childhood that she probably wouldn't remember anyway.

The frail woman lying in the bed woke up slowly and lay watching the young girl stare out the window. What was she doing here? Did she come of her own accord? She truly regretted not getting to know the child when she first came to live with her but she had a full social calendar and had no time to raise a child. Besides she was not very good with children because when she had given birth to her son, his father took over the raising of him.

She smiled as she remembered when Jackson was born. Earl had been such a history buff and was enthralled with President Andrew Jackson that he wanted to name his son after him. They ended up calling him Jack and she was just as glad because she didn't share Earl's knowledge of history. He was a president and a fairly good one, so it was said. She did love her son and he brought her great pleasure except for when he contracted the measles at the age of sixteen. That was very hard on him and he almost didn't make it through them. He was in a lot of pain for months after he had them.

He had gone to school with Caroline, from the youngest age they were inseparable. Either, she was at his house or he was at hers. They were always doing something together. When he wanted to marry Caroline, God knows, she had tried to talk him out of it but they had eloped and gotten married anyway. She had wanted him to marry into a more prominent family but in the end Jack had known best. They were so happy and in love from the very beginning and worked together in all things.

She missed her son very much and Caroline was much like a daughter to her. It happened so fast that she could never adjust to the fact that they were gone. She would never see her son again. After losing Earl, Jack was all she had. Now there was no one left in her family except for this young woman who sat faithfully beside her bed.

Faelynn looked down to see her grandmother lying there watching her. She smiled as she reached for her hand, "How are you feeling today grandmother? I hope you slept well."

She fluffed the pillow behind her and helped her turn over in the bed. "I wanted to come early today because I have to be at the house all afternoon. The repairman is coming to fix the back steps. They are in bad need of repair. The young man is out back mowing the grass right now and will be picking up the debris from the yard. It should be back to normal by tomorrow. The steps are going to take longer as he has two jobs before us." The grandmother didn't' say anything just listened to her talk about the house as if she had lived there all her life.

Faelynn sat back down in the chair, "Grandmother, I'd like your permission to change some things around the house especially the curtains in the rooms. They have been there since I was a small girl and I'm sure they are well worn by now. I'd like to get the porches repainted and a few other things I have been looking at. I won't change anything if you don't want me to but I hope you allow me to do some of it." Her grandmother narrowed her eyes and looked at her granddaughter, "Why would you want to change anything? You haven't' lived there in years. What do you care about that old house?"

She was surprised to hear her grandmother talk like that. She loved that old house. When she lived there it was because she felt unwanted. She was a grown woman now and didn't need to feel wanted by this woman but would like to make the house more cheerful when its owner returned to it.

"When my parents used to bring me to the old house I loved it. It was like a mystery to me and I wanted to explore it." Faelynn looked at her grandmother while waiting for the answer. Finally, the woman looked at her and waved her hand in dismissal, "Do what you want to the house, it will be yours soon enough anyway."

Faelynn was alarmed at how her grandmother spoke about dying. She knew she wanted to bring a subject up and didn't know exactly how to do it without upsetting her grandmother. "Grandmother, whatever happened to the Davis's that lived down the street from us? Weren't you and her close and in a lot of the clubs around town?" Her grandmother huffed, "Some friend she turned out to be, stabbed me in the back when I wasn't looking."

She looked at her grandmother with many more questions in mind, "Why do you say that? I thought she was your best friend?" Her grandmother turned her head away and stopped talking at all. She could see a sadness come over her face. Now she wondered what really happened to cause her grandmother such grief and for her to quit all activities with the town organizations. She was going to have to look into this further and if her grandmother wouldn't tell her then someone else would.

She stood beside her grandmother's bed when she was about to leave. She watched her look out the window in thought. "Is there anything I can bring you when I return? I'm going home to check on the workers and what they are doing. I will come back tomorrow early. I have a little shopping to do today. I forgot how warm it gets here and I didn't bring the right clothes. Oh, I meant to tell you that Mrs. Jones called when she saw a light on at the house and wanted to know who was there. I told her not to worry that I would be there for some time. She wishes you great speed in getting well." Her grandmother acted like she hadn't even heard her speaking. She patted her hand and walked out the door. She didn't know that her grandmother's eyes followed her.

Faelynn left the parking lot and went to the mall to look for a few clothes to get her through a week or two. It had turned very warm and dresses were too hot to wear in this weather. She was going to be working on the house and yard while she was here.

After looking at several racks of clothes she found several pair of shorts with tops that would do her well. She stopped again by the grocery store to pick up a few more things for meals. She arrived home to find the young man doing her yard still hard at work. He looked like he had been sweating, "Would you like a glass of tea or Lemonade?" He stopped and looked at her, "Thank you but water will be fine." She went inside the house and came back with a glass filled with ice cubes and cold water.

He stopped and took the glass and drank most of it down in one gulp. He let out a breath of satisfaction as the cold water hit his mouth with a splash. He finished the glass and handed it back to her, "Thanks so much that hit the spot. I'm almost done for today so I will be leaving within the hour. I should be back early tomorrow to finish up."

She started walking back to the house when the blue truck pulled up at the edge of the curb. He took steps two at a time as he reached her. She looked at him from head to toe and that eerie feeling came back to her, "Hello again," He nodded his head holding out a piece of paper to her, "Good afternoon. I finished the estimate and thought I'd drop it by so you could look it over. He handed her a paper with an estimate of what the steps would cost."

He stood watching her, as she looked it over. She was very pretty with silky blond hair and deep blue eyes with a fair completion sprinkled with freckles across the nose. She had a nice figure to boot, in her cream shirt and brown slacks. He almost whistled under his breath but kept his mouth shut tight. He wouldn't mind doing this job for nothing if she would be walking around the yard keeping him company.

She thought the estimate was very high for fixing two or three steps; perhaps she should look for another carpenter and get another bid. She looked up at him and was surprised to find him stating right into her eyes. She mumbled something about the price then caught herself.

She gathered her nerve and knew that her next words would throw him off center because he expected to get this job easily, "I have another company coming to look at them tomorrow because it is my grandmother's house I want to try to find the most reasonable cost. I do appreciate your dropping this off and I will get back with you once I get the second one."

She thanked him for giving his bid and started to walk toward the house. He yelled at her as she turned to climb the steps. "Call me if he gives you a lower bid. We can work something out about the price." She smiled and climbed the stairs and went into the house, closing it behind her. He watched her and cursed all the way back to his truck. He didn't know she was having someone else bid it too or he would have put a lower price. He could have done it a half price as it was.

Now, that she had told him a lie, she had to get the phone book and check for another carpentry company to give her, another bid. She looked under the business side and found a company called Helms Brother's Carpentry and Cabinetmakers Company. Why hadn't she noticed that the last time she looked in the book? She wondered if it could be Richard and his brother, Jackie's business. Now, the question is, should she call him. What if it is Richard? Well, a lot of time had passed and she really needed those steps fixed. She dialed the number and spoke with Jackie, the younger brother of Richard.

She explained her problem then inquired, "Can you or someone from your company come out to my grandmother's house and give me a bid on fixing her back porch steps?" Jackie informed her, "Of course, we can do it and probably in record time. One of the crew foremen will be out there this afternoon to look at it. He can give you a bid while he is there. Going into summer our work-load increases, but as long as it is still spring and when the rains come a lot, it interrupts the job. We can catch it between rains as long as it is not a lengthy repair."

She felt relieved and gave him the address, "That is great; I'll look for your foreman, what was his name again?" Jackie looked at his register for one of the foremen's name, "John

Cameron's crew." She thanked him and hung up the phone. She went into the kitchen and got her a cold glass of tea and walked back to the table where her pen and pad waited.

Maybe she could deal with Richard's company without him even knowing it. She would rather not have to deal with him directly or otherwise. They're last meeting hadn't been a pleasant one. She felt sure he probably wouldn't even remember it. He was probably married now and had a bunch of kids following him around.

Her daydreams kicked in again and she wondered what he would look like now. She found it hard to believe that she had such a crush on him when they were in school. She shook herself and exclaimed, "No, I don't want to think of him or anything else about him. I shouldn't have let Jackie even come out here to give her a bid. She could have taken Steven's bid and let him fix it." That did make her shudder. For some reason she did not like Steven or the way he looked at her. She felt like she was a bug under a magnifying glass.

She made a few notes about the house and some things she would like to either repaint or wall paper. The kitchen needed remodeling very badly. It needed some new and up to date appliances, new counter tops and most definitely new cabinets.

She heard the grass cutter shut off and knew that David was leaving. She walked out to say goodbye to him. She looked around the yard and what a difference it had made. The lawn was nice and even and the brush had been moved. The flowerbed had been weeded and all of the excess grass had been bagged and put into the garbage bag for the trash man.

She exclaimed, "David, it looks wonderful." She turned to give it a closer inspection and couldn't find one twig left on the grass. She was duly impressed with his work, "Thank you for doing such a good job. If you need a reference have them call me please." He grinned, "I'm glad you like it and I hope you remember me again when it needs a manicure." She handed him the check, "I surely will and again thanks." She turned to walk back to the house.

CHAPTER 3

She was standing on the porch when a white pickup truck stopped at the curb and the sign on the side read, "Helms Carpentry and Cabinets." She groaned inside at the thought of Richard and their last meeting. She hoped this wouldn't happen each time she saw their truck. She scolded herself; *quit being such a silly goose.* This is business and it doesn't matter who does it, as long as it gets done.

The driver of the truck stepped outside and walked toward her. She stepped down to meet him. She put out her hand and introduced herself, "My name is Faelynn Myers. My grandmother owns this house and the back porch steps are getting rickety, so I'd like an estimate of how much it would take to repair or replace them."

The tall young man with carrot top hair and a lanky style about him; stuck out his hand and took hers into it. He smiled down at her and gave her his name, "I'm John Cameron and I can look at the steps and give you some idea what it will cost to be repaired." They walked back around the house and John looked the steps over. He pushed and pulled and tried to determine how sturdy they were or if they would need total replacement. He scratched his chin and looked back at Faelynn.

He removed his ball cap hat and wiped his forehead with his arm, "Well, it looks like the steps are sturdy, even though a couple are broken. They still seem to have been built firm.

It looks like you could get away with just fixing the two steps and that can be done at a very reasonable rate."

He took a pad out of his back pocket and wrote a figure on it and handed it to her. She looked at the paper then him in surprise, "How can that be? This is more than reasonable. Are you sure this is right? When can you start?" John stared at her and smiled, "Well, let's start at the first question. I was told by my boss to do this job as reasonable as possible and I pay attention to my boss. Second question was, "Yes, it is more than reasonable but it is not so cheap, the price covers all the cost of lumber and labor. Now, I can start this afternoon and be done by tonight if that is okay with you and we have a deal on the price."

Faelynn looked at John and asked pointedly, "This is not being done as a charity case is it? Who is your boss and why would he ask you to do this as reasonable as possible?" John began to squirm as he said, "Richard, is my boss and he said that this lady is a very nice woman and is elderly and could use a break in the price. So there you have it. Do I have the job?"

She looked up into his big blue eyes and knew he was telling the truth, "Yes, you have the job and John, Thank you very much. My grandmother is in the hospital and I'm trying to get the place fixed up before she comes home." He nodded his head and walked back to his truck to get the lumber to fix the steps.

Faelynn watched him for a few minutes and walked toward the front of the house to do some laundry for her to wear back to the hospital tomorrow. She needed to talk to Dr. Wellington again about her grandmother's condition.

She arrived at the hospital a few minutes before visiting hours in hopes she would be able to talk to Dr. Wellington.

She must have timed it just right because as she had reached the revolving door going in when she saw Dr. Wellington coming out. She called to him and he stopped and turned to her. She saw a worried look on the very handsome face of her grandmother's doctor.

She realized that she hadn't really paid attention to his looks, only a general look of his handsome features. He must have been at least six feet with black hair and beautiful crystal blue eyes with that jutted chin and high cheekbones. Handsome, really didn't cover his looks; knockout, dreamboat and Rudolph Valentino, Clark Gable and Earl Flynn handsome, came to mind.

He slowly smiled at her with his bright white teeth, "Faelynn, you wanted to speak to me?" She blushed, at being caught staring at his face in a dream state. She pointed toward the bench, "Can we sit for a minute. I have a few questions about my grandmother?" He looked at his watch and replied, "Okay, for a few minutes, but I have an important meeting in twenty minutes across the campus."

They found their bench and Faelynn's expression grew worried. "Dr. Wellington, how long do you think my grandmother can last on this starvation path she is on? Is there a way to force her to eat? How can I bring her out of this slump and make her know that life is worth living again?"

Dr. Wellington rubbed his chin as he thought of a solution to her problem. He put his hand on her shoulder as he spoke, "I think your grandmother has lost the will to live because of her split with her close friends, some of them she has had for most of her life. If you try to find out what happened and see if it can be repaired then it might make her want to live again. There is another solution that might work also. If you confront her about it and threaten her with having a feeding tube put in if she doesn't start eating today. There is no way of knowing if either will work but at least we would have given it a try."

Faelynn thought for a minute turning those answers over in her mind, "Do you have time to go back to her room for me to talk to her about it. I promise it won't take more than ten minutes of your time." He looked at his watch again, stood up, "Let's go." They both walked back inside the hospital and took the elevator up to her room.

She didn't know what she was going to say to her grandmother, but it had to be done, to stop this nonsense of her refusing to eat. When they arrived at her room, the doctor took a seat and let Faelynn do the talking.

She cleared her throat as she looked down at her grandmother wasting away to nothing, in front of her eyes. She had to say something that would stop her from dying needlessly. She realized that her grandmother did mean something to her and she needed her to stay alive until they could work it out.

Faelynn took her chair beside the frail aging woman and reached out to hold her hand. The woman looked at their hands together and then to the young woman sitting beside her. Faelynn started to speak, "Grandmother, I came to talk to you about something very serious and it has been on my mind for the last few days. I find that I am not happy with my thoughts and we need to talk about them. I know, we were not close while I lived at your house and I'm not sure why. But I would like to have the opportunity to try to work it out with you if you would like the same thing."

Her grandmother just stared at her not sure what to make of this child that was now coming into her life. She was not sure what she was asking of her. Did she want to build a relationship at this late date? It was not her fault, not any of it. She was the one that made all the mistakes and wrong choices, not her granddaughter. She looked at her granddaughter holding her hand again.

Faelynn continued talking to her grandmother, "I know that you have deliberately been starving yourself in hopes of dying, but I hope and pray that you won't do that anymore. I want you to get well and come home and live there again with me. If you will start eating today, I will contact my job and resign and move here permanently to live.

Will you be willing to do that for me, for us? So we might start over as grandmother and granddaughter?" The aging grandmother looked at her granddaughter suspiciously, "Now, why would you want to move back here with me? You have your whole life ahead of you and your career to think of. You don't need to be bothered with me hanging around your neck. I think you should go on back to Oregon to your own life and let me go. I have done nothing for you; I have never been the grandmother you needed. I just can't see you dropping out of your life to take care of me."

Faelynn stared at her grandmother, "Well, that was true but you are my only living relative in this whole world and I want to be with you now that you need me. However, there is one other thing that I am prepared to do if you refuse me. That is to have your doctor put a feeding tube in you to make sure you get the nourishment you need to stay alive while we talk this out. What I'm telling you grandmother is that I want you alive no matter what. My job is not as important as your living. I will stop at nothing to keep you alive. I want you to live as long and as happy as you can possibly stand of your own free will. I don't want you to kill yourself because you think no one cares about you because that would be a lie."

She looked at the doctor sitting in the chair next to the white wall and he was swallowing hard and looking down at the floor. He took his handkerchief and wiped his face with it before tucking it back into his pocket. He looked up and saw her watching him. He smiled without really trying.

Her grandmother squeezed her hand and whispered, "Oh, Faelynn, do you really mean that? You want me to live and you will stay here in Covington and live with me in that old rickety house?" Tears formed in both their eyes as Faelynn bent down to kiss her on the cheek. "I meant every word I said, grandmother."

Her eyes showed bright with unshed tears as she looked at her granddaughter. "I promise I will start eating again. I want to come back to my beloved home and I want you to live there again too. I promise you will see a new grandmother, one much better than the old one."

She couldn't' stop the tears from flowing and neither could Faelynn. They held hands for some time before Faelynn, "Grandmother, I want to talk to Dr. Wellington for a minute before he has to leave. Then, I will be back in here to visit with you a while." Her grandmother nodded and released her hand, while giving her a little smile.

Faelynn and the doctor walked to the elevator without saying a word. They crossed the lobby and out to their bench before she turned to say something to him. He reached for her and pulled her into his arms, holding her tight, "Thank you, so much for doing that. I knew this starvation thing was because she didn't think anyone loved her. This is a big relief off my shoulders. I just can't thank you enough for doing that." He pulled back and saw that there were still tears in her eyes. He quickly found his handkerchief and dried her eyes.

They sat down on the bench to talk for a minute. Faelynn spoke first, "While I was at the house, walking from room to room. I realized how much I had missed it. Even thought, I knew my grandmother didn't love me she was still my kin. I knew I had to do something to stop this path she had chosen. I will find out what happened to the ladies group and why there was such a riff between them. In the mean time she will start to eat again. That is good enough for now. The rest will come later." She paused, "I'm sure I made the right decision. She has a long time to live yet. We can turn it around for both of us."

Dr. Wellington put his hand on her shoulder, "I wish more families were like you. I'm so glad I called you before it was too late to be reversed. Thank you for coming and for today, it has renewed my beliefs that families are everything. I really have to make that meeting so I will see you tomorrow?" She nodded, as he briskly walked away with a new spring to his step. She smiled at him as he started to run to the next building. I hope I didn't keep him too long that it made him miss the meeting. She signed. Her grandmother was so lucky to have such a doctor as him. She admired him for the way he cared for the patient and their families. Why else would he have sent for her to come home right away?

She went back up to the fourth floor and to the nurse's station and asked for a light meal for her grandmother to hold her over until lunch. The nurse informed her that her grandmother had already ordered something be brought to her room. Faelynn smiled and thanked her. When she entered the room her grandmother was sitting up in bed with a tray on the small table near her. She gave an impressive smile at her granddaughter while laughing, "I thought I should begin right away because I have a lot of catching up to do."

Faelynn gave a sigh of relief at seeing the joy on her grandmother's face, "I think we both have a lot of catching up to do." She sat down beside her and they talked between her eating the sandwich she had ordered. Faelynn felt such relief, knowing now that her grandmother was really going to try to get well. She said a silent prayer for the help and support that guided her through this ordeal.

Faelynn watched her grandmother while she took several bites of her ham and cheese sandwich with relish. "Grandmother, can you tell me why all your friends deserted you? I know it will be hard but we have to talk about it sometime. You were always involved in so many organizations and had someone at the house all the time. I can't imagine what could have come between you and them to cut it off so quickly. Can you please tell me about it?"

Her grandmother shrugged her shoulder as if it didn't mean anything to her anymore but did comment, "I guess I figured out that those so called "friends," really weren't my friends at all. The only reason they were my friends was in hopes of gaining a position of substance in town. Most of them coveted my position that I had worked so hard to get. I was in the powder room at one of the social functions when I happen to overhear my best friend, Blanch Walters tell another friend, Beth Evers that she thought I was getting too old to be the chairwoman and they should elect a younger woman who had new ideas on how to take the club further within the community.

She told her that the only reason I was still the chairperson was that I was having an ongoing affair with the President of the men's division, Randall Morrison. Randall is a dear friend of mine and has been since before my Earl died. His wife passed soon after Earl and we just bonded since that time forward. There never has been anyone before my Earl or after that would have interested me into another marriage. Earl was like a breath of fresh air, when he was in the room. He made the whole world brighter and happier. He encouraged me to fulfill my obligation to the community in our name and never complained when it took a lot of my time.

To say the least, hearing that gossip hurt me grievously and I was never able to forgive either one of them. These were two women whom I thought were my best friends and they thought nothing of stabbing me in the back. I resigned my post immediately and never went to another meeting. Several of the other ladies did ask, why I had quit so hastily but I never spoke of what I had heard those two gossip mongers. I was quite satisfied to learn that neither of them were ever elected to my post and eventually quit the club too. Randall came to see me too. He had heard the gossip and wanted to apologize to me for those women. I explained to him; it wasn't his fault and he would always remain my true friend. He is a dear man whom I enjoy being around very much. He does stop by when he can or when he's able. But as far as the rest of them I don't care one whit to speak to any of them ever again."

Well, Faelynn had gotten her answer at last. Now, she knew why her grandmother had turned her back on the social scene in Covington. It had to hurt a great deal to do that. After all the time she had spent giving of her time and talents to this community she understood the hurt and depression she had suffered.

She leaned forward so her grandmother could hear, "Grandmother, I'm so sorry you were made to suffer that humiliation. But I want you to know, they were wrong, you were not too old to serve on their committees. You were the best thing they had going for them and they were too blind to see it."

Her grandmother smiled at her for a long moment before saying, "Thank you for thinking I was doing the right thing.

I do appreciate your kindness to me." Faelynn squeezed her hand as she smiled, "I have to go now because someone is coming to fix the back porch steps and I want to see them and give them a check before they leave. I'll be back tomorrow. Be sure to eat a good supper so you can tell me all about it." She kissed her on the cheek then walked out the door.

Her grandmother smiled at the thought of getting to know her granddaughter again. Maybe she can make up for some of the time they lost, while they both grew up. She realized how lucky she was to get this chance. She would do her best to make it right this time.

Faelynn arrived back home just as John was putting his tools back into his truck. She stopped and waved at him as she got out of her car. She walked back to the porch and to her surprise all of the steps had been replaced. She looked at him with questioning eyes, "Was something else the matter with them? I see you replaced them all and not just the two that were broken."

He brushed his hands on his pants and muttered, "Yeah, well, I got to looking at the old wood and wondered how much longer they might last before they also broke so I felt it was important to replace them all for your own safety. Sometimes it's best to do that rather than take a chance to falling through another one and having to do it all over again."

She asked the carpenter, "How much more is this going to add to the bill? He looked at her and could easily see how his boss could be interested in her because she was a beautiful woman. He just gave her a lopsided smile, "Not one more penny. The satisfaction of knowing you and your grandmother are safe here is well worth the cost." She looked at him for a minute and wanted to ask why he would care if they were safe or not but she knew he was a kind of man that made a good neighbor and would care about two single women living alone. She smiled up at him and placed her hand on his arm, "Thank you John, I appreciate it very much. I guess I'm lucky my grandmother didn't break her neck falling down these stairs." She walked up them and went into the house to get his check. She went back out onto the porch and handed him his check. He took the check from her hand, "Thank you very much and if you need something else done be sure to call me." She smiled at him as he stepped off the porch and walked to his truck.

CHAPTER 4

Faelynn had fixed her dinner and was washing up the dishes when she heard a banging at the back door. It sounded as if someone was pounding the door loudly. She couldn't imagine who could be so disturbing. She opened the back door to see Steven Smith standing there about ready to explode. His face was red with anger and he looked at her as if he could kill her right there on the spot.

"Mr. Smith, is there a problem?" He open and closed his fists several times before he spoke. She was beginning to become alarmed. He spoke in an angry gravelly voice. "I thought I told you if their bid was lower than mine that I would reduce the price to match theirs. Why didn't you call me back after they gave you their bid?"

Faelynn looked at him for a moment before replying, "Mr. Smith, I am not obligated to call you if I get a lower bid. The man fixed it right them and I didn't have to wait for two days until you had the time. The choosing of the bid was my call and I chose to have it done today. Now, if you will please leave my home or should I call the police to assist you off my property?"

His face turned beet red and he mumbled before he stepped down from the porch. "You'll pay for this. I told you I'd do it and you should have called me back. After all you owe it to me, I came out here first." He stomped off the porch and all the way to his truck he mumbled and shook his fist at her.

She was getting alarmed at how unstable he was acting. She thought perhaps she should call Jefferson Carpentry and let them know how he handled himself today.

She closed the door and locked it behind her; walking into the front room she did the same and cut on the outside light for the porch. She walked back to the table when the phone rang. She picked it up to hear a familiar voice saying, "Hello." She knew it was Michael. She had tried to prepare herself for this phone call but without success. "Hello Michael, How have you been doing?" He hesitated for a minute then laughed saying, "I called to see when you were coming back this way? I thought you had taken a two week vacation?" He must have heard that she called the company asking for a few extra weeks of her vacation time.

She sighed as she tried to think of something to tell him, "I had, but it looks like it might be more like a month or more now. My grandmother is improving but slowly. The doctor says it will take time for her to get herself steady again. I called the office today to see if I could get a leave of absence for a while or at least until she improved." Michael was silent again. "Well, if you stay longer are you sure she will be up and around in that time, so you can come back to Oregon to work? "She knew what he was thinking that he would have to wait all that time for her to decide what she was going to do. "I sure hope so Michael. It's a lot harder on older people to get back on their feet than it is a young person like me."

He changed the subject and talked about some of the things happening at the office and asked her about a file she had and he needed to see the file because he was working some of her accounts. She agreed to get the file in the mail the next day. She had hoped to be back to work by now but since she knew she wouldn't then she would at least send him the file to work.

She listened to him for a few minutes and then decided it was time to go to bed, "Michael, I have to get off the phone now as it is around eleven o'clock here. The time difference is about four hours and I have to get to the hospital early tomorrow. Be sure to say hello to everyone for me and I'll be back as soon as possible. Thank you for calling and asking about my grandmother." He muttered something and then the phone went dead.

She stood there for a long time, thinking about their situation and her job and what to do about it. Quit now or hold off as long as possible. She could have all her stuff packed and shipped to her. Her apartment was furnished so there was no furniture involved. One or two of her friends could go over and pack for her. But by waiting she could use up some of her sick time and vacation time she had not used in six years. She walked over to the door and cut off the light and started up the stairs.

The house was quiet and the only thing you could hear in the neighborhood was a dog barking now and then. She had stepped on the second step of the stairs when she heard a car door slam somewhere outside. It didn't bother her because people came and went all times of the day and night. She then heard steps outside her house close to the back porch. Then she heard them stepping on the steps, she was becoming alarmed. Who could that be?

She stopped and listed to see if she could hear anything else and she heard someone shaking the screen door trying to pull it open. She had locked the screen when she had come in. She quietly stepped down the two steps and walked over to the phone where she called the police. She gave them her address and told them that someone was on her back porch trying to get inside.

They told her they would be right out because one patrol car was on the next street and he could be there in two minutes. They wanted her to stay on the phone but she told them she wanted to peek out to see what she could see or if she could recognize the person at her back door.

She went to the window and looked out over her side yard. She could see a dark truck parked just beyond her house. She couldn't see anything else it was so dark. She jumped when she heard someone turning the knob on her back door. Evidently they had gotten past the screen door. Within a few seconds she heard the window crash and someone wiggling the lock. She ran into the kitchen and picked up a knife and fled up the stairs to her room. She closed all three doors and locked hers. She stood with the knife in front of her waiting to see if the person made it to her room before the police got there.

It seemed like forever after she had heard the back door being opened. But no one had come near her room. After a few seconds she heard someone calling her name. She didn't recognize the voice. Then he identified himself as Officer Wayne Chastain. She dropped her knife and opened the door and he stood there with his hand on his gun. It was a very large and tall man who looked like he could take on the world. He looked at her shaken state while asking, "Miss Myers?" She was pale and shaken almost on the verge of tears. He put his arm around her and pulled her close to him to calm her. "Did you find the person who broke into my house?"

The officer looked around her room to be sure she was alone, "Do you live here alone? He slowly walked her down the steps and stopped at the bottom. We found a man inside the house but we need to know if you can identify him for us. Do you think you're strong enough to do that?" She shook her head *yes* and he walked her into the kitchen because the man was sitting at her table. She took one look at him and cried," Mr. Smith, why in the world would you break into my home like this? I explained to you why I accepted the other company's bid and not yours. Our conversation was over this afternoon when you stormed off my property."

The man at the table looked up at her with a mask that made him look like the devil, "Oh, Miss Myers, I know your kind of woman. You display yourself to a man in hopes that he will pay attention to you or give you special favors. You flirted with me in hopes we could trade your work for my desires." Faelynn's mouth dropped open, she was so shocked she put her hand over her mouth and quickly sucked in her breath at his bitter words.

Since Faelynn had not gone to bed she still had on her daytime clothes. The officer noticed, "Miss Myers, is this the outfit you had on today?" She looked down at her slacks and short sleeve shirt, "Yes." He reached down to help the man in handcuffs up from the chair, "Thank you, we'll be taking Mr. Smith down town so he can be processed into jail for breaking and entering."

The other officer took his arm and walked him out toward the steps and he yelled as he was being taken out the door. "They can't keep me there, I haven't done anything wrong. I'll be out on bail in two hours and I'll be back. You're not going to get off this easy. You owe me." Then he shouted as he went down the steps. "You owe me big time, lady."

Faelynn looked at the officer with large, scared eyes, "Will he really be out in two hours?" The officer put his hand on her shaking arm and corrected the man's statement, "Not when I add threatening bodily harm and assault to his file. I think that he will be in there until his trial; I'm hoping that the prosecutor will see how violent he can be and put him through a battery of tests.

They will also check to see if there are any other charges that have been filed against him. If you need me just call the center and they'll dispatch a car right out. This is usually my beat so it probably will be me. Don't worry; I think he's going to regret threatening you this time, no telling how many other women he has done this too. I am going to send an officer out to stay in the yard tonight until you can get someone to fix that back door." She gave a sigh of relief, "Thank you again for coming so quickly, and for security tonight." He tipped his hat to her and she heard him as he walked out the door ask the police center for an officer to be with her tonight.

She thought to herself, *oh great, I've only been here two weeks and already someone doesn't like me. I'm off to a great start. I wonder whom I can get to fix the back door. Guess I could call John to see how much he will charge me to do it.* She went up to her room to change into her nightclothes and came back down to fix her a hot cup of tea to help her sleep. She noticed that there was a police car sitting in her back yard already. She felt so much better. The Covington police were right on the ball when she called them. Thank goodness that nut case didn't get up to her room. She didn't know what she would have done had he came through her bedroom door.

She took her tea and went to the living room to sit so her nerves would calm down. She was going to be late getting to the hospital tomorrow she knew that for sure. No sense mentioning this to her grandmother and upsetting her, which would be of no benefit.

As she sipped her tea she tried to think of a reason Mr. Smith would have of singling her out to personally attack. She knew he was upset over not getting the bid for the steps but his was so high it didn't make sense to pay that for his services. What other reason could he have, was it because she was a single woman living alone. He thought he could bully her into paying his high price and then allow him to maul her for sexual favors.

Her mind could not comprehend his thinking. No woman in her right mind would even want to be around him. He gave her the willies because he was so creepy. But bullying and threats seemed to be his style. Thank goodness for quick police officers.

She took her cup back to the kitchen and rinsed it out. She peeked again outside and saw the police car sitting there. She sighed and knew she had been a lucky woman that night and was grateful for the kindness of the police department.

Once she reached her room she looked on the floor for the knife she had brought up from the kitchen. She laid it on her nightstand and crawled into bed hoping for a peaceful night. She drifted off to sleep finally but had several disturbing dreams that made her toss and turn.

She woke the next morning with a slight headache and couldn't seem to get rid of the muddled feeling she had from lack of sleep. She went down to fix her breakfast and noticed the police car still there. She stepped out onto the porch with a cup of coffee in hand. The police officer opened his door and walked up to take it from her. "I wasn't sure if you used cream or sugar but I have both if you would like them in the coffee."

He replied, "No, black is fine and thanks for thinking of me." He sat down on the steps to drink his fresh cup of coffee. She offered him breakfast but he refused saying his shift ended in a few minutes and he would be heading home.

She made herself a cup of cereal with toast and sat at the table eating when the phone rang. "Hello." The voice on the other end was her boss, Mr. Webb. He had gotten the report that she had requested more time off from his accountant. She had the time but he wanted to see how things were going. "So, Faelynn, how is your grandmother doing?" She was surprised to hear from him because she had spoke with the personnel office and they had assured her that she had a few weeks accumulated she could use. "Good Morning Mr. Webb, She is doing better but just barely. She seems to have let herself get run down. Her doctor said it would be a slow process getting back on her feet. I contacted the personal office yesterday to see how much vacation I had and they had told me at least two more weeks. Is that a problem Mr. Webb?" Her boss hesitated then said, "Well, I guess not since you do have the time coming. It's just that we're busy and everybody is needed to handle the accounts."

Faelynn felt guilty for taking so much time off because she knew the office was busy this time of year. "I'll be back as soon as she is out of the hospital and can handle her affairs. Hopefully, that should take more than the time I asked for." Her boss still didn't sound satisfied. "I guess we will just have to wait and see then. See you in a few weeks and hope your grandmother gets better soon."

Well, she was glad that phone conversation was over. She was biding her time to use some of her days up before she resigned. She reached for her briefcase and looked through it to see what other files she had with her. She found two more and found an envelope to put them in as she addressed them to Michael with a note explaining she would be here for another two weeks and that she was sure he might needs these files. She apologized for such a delay getting back but that the doctor was monitoring her grandmother's progress and it was going very slow. They were trying to build her strength back up by giving her milk shakes and special food to help her gain strength.

She laid the envelope by the door so she didn't forget to take it with her to the post office to mail. She also checked the number for John and called the company as soon as it was opened. She didn't recognize the voice that answered the phone but asked for John. The voice on the end of the line asked, "May I ask who is calling? Is this a business or personal call?" She quickly replied so that they would not think that it was personal.

"This is Faelynn Myers, I had a burglary at my home last night and he broke my back door and it needs to be repaired quickly. I had hoped he might find time to do it today. I don't mind paying him if he can. Could you have him call or stop by this morning?" The voice said, "Yes, I'll put the note in his mailbox to work on today." Faelynn felt relief and hoped that he might get there early to fix the door, "Thank you very much and please mark it urgent." The phone disconnected but she hoped the person heard her and did ask him to come out to her house as quickly as possible.

She ran upstairs to shower before he arrived. She wanted to get to the hospital at least by noon but wasn't exactly sure she would be able to do that. After dressing and brushing her hair for some time she came back down stairs and saw John looking at the back door. She walked over to greet him. "Hello John, Isn't it a mess?" He stopped to look at her in bewilderment, "What did you do to get this banged up?" She thought about what he said, did he think she did this? "I had a man come out and give me a bid on the back porch steps and he got mad when I asked you to do it." He looked shocked, "You're kidding, right. Who the heck was it, someone local?"

She nodded her head then told him, "It was a man from Jefferson Carpentry. He came out and gave me a very high bid. Wait, I still have it." She went to the desk drawer and pulled it out and took it back to him. He took the paper and looked at it and scratched his head. "Why in the world would he charge so much money for fixing those steps? They didn't need to be replaced totally." She then told him of what Mr. Smith had said to her and the police officer. "He seemed to think that he could barter the steps with sexual favors from me." He stopped and looked at her for a long time before saying, "Lady, are you sure? Things like that don't happen in small friendly towns like ours."

She snatched her paper back, insulted that he thought she might be lying about the reason the door was busted up, "Well, it did and there is a police report about it and the police officer heard him threaten me again." John just shook his head in disbelief while scratching his few whiskers, "I'll get right on this because you need this lock replaced and done by tonight. So you can feel safe in your home again.

After telling him that she had to go to the hospital very quickly she left him to work by himself. She felt a little miffed that he had questioned her about the situation almost like he didn't believe her. She had never had anything like this happen before and she surely didn't make a mistake on how it took place.

She drove straight to the hospital and met Doctor Wellington again at the door. They sat in their usual place and talked for a while. She explained her delay in getting to the hospital, "I've had a little trouble at the house and someone busted in the back door. Some carpenter that I rejected his bid to fix our steps and he got mad and wanted revenge.

The other thing you need to know is my boss called from Oregon checking on how my grandmother is doing. He might call you directly because I think he's getting suspicious because I'm staying here so long. He knows I wouldn't have stayed here that long before. I just wanted to give you a heads up to warn you if he should contact you." The doctor put his hand on her arm and squeezed it gently, "Faelynn, are you alright? Did the guy hurt you in any way? Let me know if I can do anything for you, will you?"

She nodded her head and stood up to go into the hospital. "Don't worry about your grandmother, she is doing much better." She thanked him and walked to the revolving door.

She walked into the room to see an elderly man sitting in the chair next to her grandmother. She smiled and put her things on the small counter next to the window. She waited for her grandmother to introduce them. The frail woman looked from the man to her granddaughter, "Faelynn, this is my good friend, Randall Morrison. I have known him and his late wife since before Earl had died. Randall, this is my granddaughter, Faelynn. She belonged to my son and his wife Caroline." Randall extended his hand but did not offer to stand. Faelynn knew that he was in bad shape too and probably had help getting to the hospital.

She spoke to the gentleman as she reached to take his hand in hers, "Mr. Randall, I have heard good things about you. Do you live in our neighborhood?" He cleared his throat before replying, "No, I live on the other side of town. I have a housekeeper that helps me get around, when I wish to visit Laura." He knew that would be one of her questions and answered it before she could ask.

Faelynn looked at her grandmother, "I would like to run down to the cafeteria for a cup of coffee, if you will excuse me grandmother. It is so nice to meet you Mr. Morrison." She walked to the elevator and pushed the level one button. She found the cafeteria and ordered a cup of coffee. She walked back to the end of the cafeteria and watched the activity in the room. She saw many nurses and doctors stop for their meals or just to have a cold drink. Four of the nurses sat at a table near her and talked all through their lunch. She had brought a book to read in case grandmother was asleep or to give her time to visit with her friend. She was glad that she had kept in touch with such a dear friend.

She tried to concentrate on her reading but the nurses were laughing a lot and she wondered what was so funny. She glanced up to see Dr. Wellington standing at the door looking around at the tables. The nurses at the next table all sucked in their breath at the sight of him. She peeked over the top of her book and saw him coming right straight to her table. She smiled and wondered what the nurses were thinking now. They were almost drooling. He stopped and she looked up. He laughed and smugly said, "So, we meet again. May I join you Faelynn?" She motioned for him to take a seat, "Of course," and she smiled back at him.

She caught a glance at the next table and all eyes were wide and their mouths dropped open. She laughed to herself. She folded her book closed and laid it aside. She smiled as he took the seat next to her instead of on the opposite side of the table, "Did you stop for coffee?" He smiled back at her then, he lay his folder on the table, "No, I just came to talk. Do you want to walk outside to our bench?" She stood and looked at the ladies at the next table and thought they might faint. She was really going to get a chuckle out of this when she got home.

He took her arm and walked with her talking as they left. "I got concerned about you after you went inside so after my next patient I thought to look you up. I'm concerned about what happened to you and if there are going to be some repercussions from the man who broke into your home." They arrived at their bench and she noticed that the nurses from the cafeteria were still looking out the window.

She looked at his hand, while it held hers, "I don't think there should be a problem but I will be on my guard from now on. The police assured me that he wouldn't be out anytime soon because they were going to charge him with breaking and entering, endangerment and bodily harm along with threatening me." Dr. Wellington reminded her, "But with today's slick lawyers, he could still get out again on bond. I want to give you my private number and if you should have any kind of problem call that number and they will page me right away."

She took his card and placed it in her pocket. "Thank you, for your concern but I'm sure it will be fine. I'd best get back upstairs. Grandmother was visiting with her friend Randall." The doctor grinned and replied, "Yes, he was there when I stopped in looking for you. He has left now. I helped him down to the housekeeper's car so she could take him back to his home. He is a very nice man and does visit when he can."

Dr. Wellington stood when she did. He placed his hand on her arm. "Remember to call me if you need me anytime day or night, I'll be there." She smiled up at him and blinked at this very kind and concerned stranger, "Dr. Wellington, you're a kind and generous man. Thank you for everything, especially for looking after my grandmother." He grinned at her and they walked back into the hospital. She went directly to her grandmother's room and sat in the chair near her. She watched her for a minute before speaking, "Grandmother I'm glad Randall was able to visit with you today. It's nice of him to stay in touch after all that has happened. He acts like such a nice gentlemen and we all know there are only a few of those left."

Her grandmother just smiled and looked out the window thinking of her last friends, "Yes, he is a nice man and a gentleman." Faelynn thought perhaps she wanted to say more but wasn't ready to give up her secret. Five o'clock came fast and Faelynn needed to get home to pay the repairman. "Grandmother, I have to leave now, I will be back tomorrow. I'm glad to see your doing better. Are they going to let you get out of bed to walk a little?" Her grandmother tried not to think of the pain she would have when they got her up to walk, "Yes, they will be getting me up tomorrow for some walking lessons. It should be fine and I will get stronger every day."

Faelynn saw such an improvement already, "Okay, I will be back first thing in the morning so I can help you walk. Have a nice night and eat a good supper. I'll see you tomorrow." She bent to kiss her on the cheek before leaving. She took the elevator down and walked to her car. She searched her purse for the keys while looking around the parking lot. She seemed to be more cautious and aware of who was around her. That was a good lesson especially after last night.

When she opened her door and got inside she hears someone running toward her calling her name. She stepped back outside the car when Dr. Wellington approached her. "Hello again, I wondered if you might want to have dinner with me tonight. I'm off and we can go someplace nice and just sit and relax." She smiled at him as she looked at his tasseled hair from his run, "Hello to you too, I'm sorry I can't tonight. I'm meeting the repairman at the house so I can give him his money for fixing my back door. Oh but, you can come to dinner at the house if you'd like. Do you want to come in about an hour?

That would give me time to freshen up and start dinner." He raised his eyebrows as if she thought he might refuse, "You can count on it." She gave him the address and he promised to be there on time. They smiled at each other before he turned to go back into the hospital. She started her car and drove home.

Upon arriving at her house not only was there two white trucks with the name Helms Carpentry and Cabinets but three or four men stood around in her yard as if waiting for her. She looked at them as she cut off her car and got out. She recognized John but didn't know who the others were. She walked up to her door and let herself inside. She came back out and walked over to John to find out how much her bill was going to be. When she approached his group she noticed one person who seemed familiar. But it couldn't be him. God she hoped it wasn't him. She thought she could deal with his company and not have to meet him at all. But her luck had run out.

She spoke to John, "Do you have a bill for me? I'm sorry to be so late but I was late getting to visit with grandmother." John looked at her and then at Richard, his boss. Richard took over the conversation and Faelynn didn't like it at all. He took her arm in his hand and started walking her toward her house, "Can we talk inside? I have some questions that perhaps you might have the answers to." She removed her arm from his hand and walked toward her front door. She stepped inside and went to the living room. She offered him a seat, "Would you like some refreshment, tea or lemonade?" He looked at her for a long time without speaking. "Yes, I'd like tea if you have some." She left to get the drinks and noticed that he followed her into the kitchen. He watched her pour their glasses, "When did you move back to Covington, Faelynn?"

She handed him his glass, "I haven't moved back here as yet. I still live and work in Portland, Oregon.

He stared at her for a moment then sat his glass on the table, "Come, and look at your newly repaired door. It is stronger than before because now it is reinforced so it will take an axe to break it now." Again, she looked at the door, "Do you have a bill so that I might pay it. It was very nice of John to get it fixed today. I do appreciate his work." They walked back to the kitchen table taking their former seats. He noticed her stiffness as an unforgiving act.

Richard sat across from her at the table as if in thought staring at her, "Why wouldn't you let me apologize for my very bad behavior at the senior prom. I felt like a heel for years after that. I felt as though I had run you out of town because of my overactive hormones." She didn't say a word just stared at him thinking, *It doesn't matter it's too late anyway.* Richard continued, "Gosh, I'm so sorry, I had hoped you would have forgiven me by now."

She waited a minute or two then replied to his question, "There is nothing to forgive. I had forgotten the incident a long time ago. I had a career to build and my schooling was the most important thing I had going for me. If you will give me the bill, I can write you a check."

Richard stood and shoved his hands in his pockets in an unsettling gesture, "There is no bill Faelynn. I feel I owe you that much as a way of apology. One I know you're never going to accept. Again, I am so sorry for such bad behavior on my part. My only excuse was that I was so in love with you and wanted you so bad I couldn't think straight. I was going to propose to you that night, but it didn't work out that way." He turned and walked out the door; she heard it slam and winced. She shouldn't have been so rude to him but she realized she hadn't forgiven him either. What would it have cost to be kinder? *Nothing, at all;* She sighed; *I guess I have a knack for messing things up.*

She sat there for a while thinking about the situation then she remembered she was having company tonight and jumped up and ran upstairs to shower. She showered and dressed and hurried back downstairs to start dinner. Just as she got the chicken and baked potatoes in the oven she heard a car in the yard. She looked out to see the doctor walking up her steps dressed in casual clothing. She opened the door before he knocked and opened her arm inviting him inside. They walked to the living room, "Would you like some tea or coffee or lemonade?" He turned and replied, "Tea sounds good; can I help you?" She looked at him and smiled, "Sure, right this way. You can check out my second new door." They walked into the kitchen and she got down the glasses as he inspected the door. "Nice job, they did with this." She laughed and turned around to hand him his glass of tea. They both stood looking at it when he turned to her, "By the way, why don't you call me Kurt. I'd feel funny if you called me Dr. Wellington when we're sharing dinner." They both laughed and that seemed to ease the tension somewhat. He walked around looking at the house, it was nice and cozy and welcoming. He commented, "This is a nice old place. Has it been in the family long?" Faelynn looked at the house that looked the same when she was a girl. She loved it then and still did; it was her father's family home. "Yes, I think it had because grandmother told me of my father growing up here and some of the things that they did when he was a young child."

They walked back to the kitchen just as the timer on the stove went off indicating that her meal was done. She fixed a salad and set the table as they made small talk about her grandmother and the town. They sat down to eat as Kurt commented. "This is nice Faelynn. I don't get much home cooking. Not, that many of the families haven't offered but their intentions were to fix me up with their daughters and granddaughters." He then laughed. Faelynn laughed but replied with a straight face. "You certainly don't have to worry about getting fixed up with me because I'm not in the market for a husband. A friend will do just fine." He watched her and smiled because that pleased him. He knew she didn't expect anything from him other than friendship. He was a young doctor and couldn't afford things like houses, cars or kids just yet. But he knew she would be a good friend to him.

They shared an enjoyable meal together and found they had quite a bit in common. They both had been lonely growing up and never seemed to fit into things such as sports or clubs in school or they were too busy studying to get ahead in their careers.

They retired to the living room after the dishes were done by both of them, because Kurt insisted he help her clean up.

They sat in the living room and talked for hours before Kurt stood, "I'd better be getting back to the hospital because I have an early shift tomorrow. You know how it is with new doctors they're loaded down with work, especially, if they live in house. It was a lovely meal and I thoroughly enjoyed the conversation. Thank you for inviting me. Next time we'll have to find a good restaurant so you don't have to cook." She laughed as she replied to his comment about her cooking. "I'll have you know I'm a good cook because I've been practicing since I too live alone." They both laughed as she walked him to the door. He kissed her on the cheek and thanked her again for a wonderful meal and good company. He walked down the stairs to his car. She locked the door and cut the porch light on.

He drove away looking at her house in his rear view mirror. He worried about her being there alone now that he saw how much trouble she had been having.

CHAPTER 5

It was visiting time at the hospital again and this time Faelynn got a very happy surprise. When she came into her grandmother's room she saw an empty bed. Thinking perhaps she had some test or other she placed the lilacs on the dressing table near the bed. The aroma they gave off into the room smelled heavenly. She walked outside to the nurse's station to see where her grandmother had gone.

She recognized one of the nurses as being with the other four in the cafeteria, who had sat at the table next to her. "Could you tell me the whereabouts of my grandmother? She isn't in her room so I though perhaps she was having a test of some kind." The nurse stared at her for a moment, "Oh now I remember, she is walking with an aid down the back hall. We've had her up three times today exercising her legs and checking out her hip, per Dr. Wellington's orders. Faelynn thought, wonderful she is trying to get better, "Oh, okay then, I'll wait in her room for her to return." The nurse smiled at her and went back to her charts.

Faelynn pulled out her book and started reading where she left off at home. She had read one or two pages when her grandmother returned to the room on the arm of an aid. The aid helped her to the bathroom and then to bed. The young girl said, "Rest some now, because we have one more walking lesson for today. Then it is shower time and to beddy bye for you. I'll be back in three hours to get you again." She nodded at Faelynn and walked out of the room.

She looked at her grandmother to see if she seemed tired or worn out from the walk. "How many times have you walked up and down the halls now, grandmother? Do they let you rest when you're tired?" Her grandmother felt a little tired but had more energy today, "Oh yes, I'm feeling better every day. I can almost walk them alone but I'm afraid I might fall, so I wait for them to come and get me." She smiled at her grandmother. She was glad to hear the good news; she is doing much better and ready to walk on her own.

They had talked for almost an hour when Faelynn told her, "I need to go on home and get some rest myself. I didn't sleep well last night and it seems to have caught up with me. I hope you don't mind grandmother. I will be back early tomorrow." Her grandmother squeezed her hand, "Of course, I don't mind, it's hard to sit in a hospital room for as long as you have. Go home and get some rest." Faelynn kissed her bye and walked out the door. Just as she reached the lobby he heard her name again coming from the cafeteria. She turned into the room and spotted Dr. Wellington sitting at a table alone. She walked over and he stood to help her into her chair. Of course, this was under the watchful eyes of about fifty nurses who were drooling at him. She smiled at him knowing she was sitting in a coveted chair, as she waited for him to tell her what he wanted.

He smiled back at her as taking in all her features. She had beautiful silky blond hair and beautiful blue eyes that looked enormous at times. He sighed indignantly, "Well, I guess you haven't had any more trouble from your carpentry man because you haven't called me screaming for help in the middle of the night." She laughed because she knew he was trying to keep it light so she wouldn't be scared over the situation. "No, it has been really quiet there. I did check with the police department and the officer said that he is not getting out anytime soon so I need not worry about him for a while. Believe me that is a big relief to me."

The doctor looked at her with his smiling eyes, "They are having a benefit dinner dance at the country club this Friday. Would you consider being my date for the night? I promise to have you home early and I can promise you a good time. Those events are always fun to attend. The music is good and I can dance, well somewhat."

They both laughed. She smiled back at him and shook her head, "Yes," "I think that sounds like a lot of fun and would love to attend something like that. I have been here for a month and haven't gone anywhere but to the hospital, grocery store and home. What time does it start and it is formal is that right?"

He pulled the paper out of his pocket and read it to her. "It starts at seven and goes until midnight. But I won't keep you out that long. The dinner is three choices, chicken, fish or steak. The benefit is for the youth summer camp that the country club sponsor's every year. It makes sure many of the kids that can't afford to go to summer camp, can go because of the money they raise there." She looked at him without saying a word. "Is that one of your favorite charities?" He blushed and whispered, "Yes, but don't tell everyone because I'd have every mother in town knocking on my door for some personal charity of their own that they want sponsored. I didn't have it so easy growing up so I like to help other kids when I can." She smiled at him and touched his arm, "You're a good man Charlie Brown." He stood up to leave but looked into her eyes, "Thank you; coming from you I know it is genuine. Pick you up at seven tomorrow night right." She shook her head "Yes." He breezed out the cafeteria door with a dozen eyes watching him including hers.

She stood to leave but sat down quickly and pulled the paper in front of her face. She peaked at the edge of it to see if she could see who was standing in the door. Yes, it was he. She would have known him anywhere and even with all the lights off. What was he doing here? Oh great, he's walking this way. She laid the paper down and reached for her purse as if she hadn't seen him. But before she could get up out of the chair he was standing right in front of her.

He put his hands on the back of the chair, "Hello Faelynn, may I sit with you for a minute?" She muttered, "I was just getting ready to go." He stared at her taking in every feature that he had memorized so many years ago, "It won't take a minute of your time, may I sit." She motioned to the chair. Richard moved his chair closer to hers under the watchful eyes of the nurses at the next table.

He looked into her beautiful face and sighed a regret from the past that still haunted him, "Faelynn, I think it is time we had a long talk about our past, to try to clear the air between us. I would love to take you out to dinner so we can discuss it. Are you free tomorrow night?" She looked at him in a strange way. Why would he care one way or the other if we were friends? It won't make a difference now it's too late. But instead she said, "No, actually I do have an engagement tomorrow. I really don't see what this is going to change Richard. I spend a lot of time with my grandmother and have for the last month. She has been very ill but seems to be on the road to recovery now."

Richard looked at her for a long time. "Can I stop by your house over the weekend so we can talk? I'd really appreciate it Faelynn. I'd like to clear the air between us and perhaps we can become friends again. At least, I think we should try to talk it out. I think it will help us both. You know what they say; there are always two sides to a story." She thought for a minute, "Sunday would be good for me. That is when I do my house chores so I'm there most of the day." He touched her arm and still felt the tingling of being near her, "Good, I'll see you early Sunday."

Another nurse was coming in to join the four already seated. She saw Richard standing at her table and walked over to him, "Good Morning Mayor Helms isn't it the most beautiful day?" Richard turned to look at Faelynn then replied to her question, "Yes, it is the most beautiful day. One like I haven't seen in a long time." He bowed his head to her and walked out the door. The nurses at the next table sighed and looked at her. She sighed too thinking of the mounting problems that seem to be coming her way. She muttered as she was leaving, "Guess, when it rains it pours." Knowing that none of them would know what it meant. She drove to the grocery store for more supplies. She was glad that her schoolmate wasn't there to ask a dozen questions from her. She checked out her few groceries and went on to her home. She was already tired and ready for an early bed. She fixed a light supper and took her glass of wine into the living room where she worked on her budget for that week. She needed to transfer some money from her bank in Oregon to here. She should go to the bank tomorrow and open an account. She wanted to stop by the dress shop to see if they had anything nice to wear tomorrow night. Short notice so she would have to take what she could get for the dinner dance. If nothing else she could wear one of the business suits she brought with her.

Faelynn got up early the next morning because there was so much to do and her mind wouldn't let her forget it. She fixed her breakfast and sat at the kitchen table making notes. It was Friday so she needed to get things in town done early. She was about to take her dishes to the sink to be washed when the phone rang. *She thought who in the world would be calling this early?*

She picked the phone up and said, "Hello." Michael was on the other end started speaking, "Good morning beautiful." She laughed touching her uncombed hair, "If you saw me this morning you'd know for sure I wasn't beautiful." They shared a good laugh, "I never saw you when you were not perfectly groomed with every hair in place and the makeup applied to perfection. Perhaps I should fly down there so I can see you in cut off jeans and a baggy sweat shirt with curlers in your hair and no makeup."

Faelynn couldn't help but laugh at that because she had never been one for baggy sweatshirts, her grandmother would have thrown a fit had she worn one. Michael changed the subject to her grandmother. "How is your grandmother doing? It's been over a month since you left here, I feel abandoned. There is no one to go with me to a dinner or a movie." Faelynn thought of how nice Michael had been to her and how sweet he was to remember special occasions. "I'm sorry Michael, I know I've been gone a long time but she is my only living relative. I have to take care of her until she is back on her feet. She's old and fragile and needs someone around her. She is doing a lot better than when I first got here thought. They have her up walking at the hospital three times a day. It tires her out some but she is struggling to do it. She is really trying hard to get better."

Michael heard the concern in Faelynn's voice and felt guilty for his petty words, "I know you're doing the best you can. I'm sorry I didn't' mean to chide you about staying gone

so long. I just missed having you around to brighten my day."
Faelynn was relieved that he didn't come right out and ask her
when she thought she would be coming home. "Michael, thank
you for your kind words, you're support and understanding.
I have to go now I have a lot to do today before I go to the
hospital." Reluctantly Michael knew she wanted to get off the
phone, "Okay, I'll talk to you another day then." She smiled
and thought he is such a nice man to be wasting his time with
me. He should be looking for a woman who is ready to settle
down and start a family with him. They said they're good by's
and she hung up the phone.

Faelynn knew that Michael was serious about her but
she wasn't ready to settle down with someone she did not
love whole-heartedly. Michael was more like a friend than
a boyfriend. She had never encouraged him to get serious;
she didn't want a serious relationship to complicate her life.
She washed her dishes and put them in the drainer to dry. She
walked up the stairs to her room with her mind still in turmoil.
She should tell Michael it's over so he won't be expecting
something of her she can't deliver. She made her bed and
picked her clothes out to wear that day. She was still thinking
about Michael when she stepped back out of the shower. She
knew then she was going to write him a letter and break their
relationship off. Michael deserved someone to love him in
return and to share his life completely.

Hopefully, before he buys a ring. She scolded herself for
letting it go this far without saying something to him about
not getting serious. The only reason she could think of as to
why she hadn't was that she was lonely or homesick one. But
now she knew what she had to do and it would be done before
Monday for sure.

She dressed and fixed her hair and applied a little makeup knowing she was going to be shopping for most of the day. She went back down stairs to pick up a little before leaving the house.

The first place she stopped was at the little boutique where they sold upscale ladies wear. She looked through the dozens of racks that were filled with dresses and formal wear. She found three she wanted to try on to see how they would fit her body. She stood in front of the mirror looking at it critically. Did it fit right? Did it hang well on her? She chose an ice blue with a low cut top and trimmed with silver. Her next stop was at the shoe section. She looked over several pair of shoes that would match the dress but settled on a nice strapped high heel that was so close to the same color it could have been made from the same dye. Satisfied with her purchases she went on to the bank to get her account settled.

She met with a loan officer to get the account opened. He reached out his hand to shake hers, "I'm so glad to meet you Faelynn. I know your grandmother well and had wondered how she was doing. I'm glad to see you're here to take care of her. It's sad when the elderly need so much assistance. They hate it because they feel unnecessary. Thank goodness you're here to be with her. Will you be moving back to the area?"

Faelynn looked at the chatty man for a few minutes before answering, "Yes, as soon as she gets better I will be going back to Oregon to close my affairs there." Mr. Davis spoke saying, "Oh, it is not necessary for you to return to close out your account we can do that for you. All we have to do is do a balance transfer and ask them to close it for you." She seemed annoyed as she replied, "I can't close my account there yet because my employer deposits my checks into it. I have not resigned my position with the company yet but I expect to

do that within the next month. I'm using vacation time now."
She was angry at his attitude. It was no business of his if she
closed her account in Oregon.

Perhaps she was angry with herself for not making a
decision on that yet. She probably should have resigned when
she figured out she wasn't going back to work. She sighed
and checked her temper toward poor Mr. Davis. She smiled at
him when he finished, "I suspect I will be looking for another
job in Atlanta, once I get settled into the house here. I still
have a lot to do either way. Thank you for taking care of my
transfer. Now, I can get some of the remodeling done on my
grandmother's home. Goodbye Mr. Davis." He stood and took
her hand in his, "Welcome back to Covington, Faelynn. It's a
pleasure to be of service to you. Anything, I can help you with
please let me know." He handed her his business card, which
she tucked into her pocket. She turned and walked out the
door to her car still in deep thought about her moving plans.
How much longer could she put it off before notifying her
boss of her decision?

She stopped by the hospital to visit a while with her
grandmother. But again she was out of her room. She stopped
by the nurse's station and was told she was walking again. She
asked the nurse on duty, "Does she seem to be getting stronger
with the walks? Do you feel she might be able to come home
soon?" The nurse that handled her mother on a daily basis
replied, "Can we step into your grandmother's room to talk?"
Faelynn followed her into the room. The nurse opened her
grandmother's folder before saying, "Faelynn, I think your
grandmother is pulling herself out of the hole she had dug to
crawl into and die.

Since you have come home she has a whole new attitude
about getting well. I don't know what you did or how you did

it but I do think your grandmother is going to get well enough to leave here and return to her home in a short time. When I come in to give her medicine, she is constantly talking about you and how happy she is that you're going to be living with her. You have given her a new lease on life. I hope that you are intending to stay with her because if you're not, then, it will crush her. She is a nice woman and seems so content now."

Faelynn couldn't keep the tears from her eyes. She dabbed them with her Kleenex, "Thank you so much. I had hoped it might have made her feel better to know I will be moving back to care for her. I didn't realize how happy it has made her though. Thank you so much, I appreciate your being so honest with me. I am moving back. It's just I have to get my things settled there and have my stuff shipped here. I'm trying to get some remodeling done and surprise her when she is able to come home." The nurse smiled at her and put her hand on Faelynn's shoulder. "You and your grandmother are going to be fine and will work out anything that is between you. Now, I'm sure of that." She turned and walked back to her desk leaving Faelynn staring after her.

Faelynn felt much better about her grandmother's exercising. Now that some of her funds had been transferred she could start remodeling her grandmother's home. Monday she would go to the hardware store and start choosing the paint for the bedrooms. She would start with them and work down.

She was standing there in her own thoughts when her grandmother walked into the room. She stared at her granddaughter wondering what she was lost in thought about. Faelynn turned around to see her grandmother standing there. She smiled and walked over to her. Taking her arm she walked her back to her bed. She smiled as she watched her get back into bed for her rest, "How are you doing? It is great to see you walking around for a change. I know you had to be getting tired of that bed." Her grandmother laughed and nodded her head in agreement, "Yes, my butt was beginning to feel like it was glued to the bed sheet." They both laughed about that.

Her grandmother brows furrowed as she looked at her granddaughter, "Faelynn, you haven't changed you mind about moving back here have you?" Faelynn looked at her in surprise. "Why no, grandmother, what made you think of that? Today I went to the bank to open an account here to have some of the funds transferred from my account there. I can't have them all transferred because my paychecks still go into that one in Oregon. To be honest, I'm trying to figure out how to break the news to my boss. Should I send him a letter of resignation or call him on the phone to tell him and follow up with a letter. So yes, I have been thinking of how to get it resolved. So I have decided that next week I am going to take care of my job, I can have my two friends go to my apartment and pack my stuff for me and ship it here or I can fly back to Portland for a day or two and hand my resignation in personally then clear out the apartment and say my goodbyes to my three friends. My boss won't be happy but there is no other way to resolve the situation. My rent is due in a month so that will be perfect timing to give notice of my moving to the apartment manager too."

Her grandmother was so happy with the news that she threw her arms around her granddaughter for the first time ever. Faelynn was so shocked she closed her arms around her grandmother too. The doctor stood at the door watching the two women embrace. He knew that this was a milestone in their lives for repairing their relationship and that he didn't want to disturb them so he stepped out of the doorway before they saw him.

He couldn't help but smile as he walked toward the nurse's station to see his next patient. He handed the folder to her and told the nurse, "Hold this file out, I'll go back and visit her in a moment. Grandmother and her granddaughter are sharing a special moment and I don't want to disturb them." The nurse didn't ask what he meant but handed him another chart and laid the other one down beside her phone. She did enjoy the smile he bestowed upon her as she saw him walking toward the station. She sighed and though of the lucky woman who would be going with him to the country club dinner-dance that night. She would have gladly accepted had he asked her. Guess she would have a secret crush on him forever. What a dreamboat.

Faelynn and her grandmother pulled away from each other. Her grandmother patted her cheek, "My dear, you have made me so happy." Faelynn looked at her for a minute, "Me too, grandmother. I know we can work everything out this time."

When the doctor appeared in the door he smiled at the two women still holding hands and talking together. This is what the elderly fragile woman had needed for a long time, and the only person who could have given it to her was the younger woman, her granddaughter.

He knocked softly, "Good morning ladies, it's time for your favorite doctor to visit." They all laughed. He helped the elderly woman to her bed as Faelynn took a seat near the window so he could examine her grandmother. He checked her pulse, took her temperature and checked her heart and asked her a few questions. "How is the walking going, I'm hearing good news from the nurses. They think in a few weeks you might be running the Boston marathon." He laughed as he held her hand. "So tell me Laura, how are you truly feeling?"

The elderly woman looked from the doctor to her granddaughter as she spoke, "I am feeling so much better that

I think I'm almost ready to leave here. I want to thank you for your concern over me and for bringing my granddaughter back into my life. So, to answer your question, I'm a very happy woman and looking forward to going home to live with my granddaughter." He smiled at her and turned to look at Faelynn who smiled back at him. He tucked her chart under his arm and stood up, "That is wonderful. I see such a big improvement in your health and your attitude about living again. I do think your time here is numbered because you're on your way to a speedy recovery." He patted her hand and turned to Faelynn, "I'll pick you up at six thirty if that is alright with you?" She nodded and he left the room. Her grandmother looked astonished at her granddaughter, "You have a date with the doctor?" Faelynn watched him walk out of the room, "It's not that big of a deal. We're having dinner for his favorite charity." She laughed, but her grandmother just looked at her. "For this small town that event is the biggest thing of the year." Faelynn wondered if her grandmother didn't want her to go but why? She smiled at her grandmother before saying, "I think it would be nice to get out of the house and go do something fun." Her grandmother smiled at her and agreed, "You have been isolated since you came back. It's nice to go out to parties and enjoy yourself some. You have yourself a good time and dance a lot and meet the many new people that will be there. Our town is growing some and we will see a whole new group of people moving into our area soon from the west." Faelynn changed the subject. She mentioned to her grandmother that she wanted to redecorate her room. It was much too childish and she wanted some different colors in it. She explained she would be going to the hardware to look over some colors and perhaps wall paper. Her grandmother listened without saying a word as if in deep thought.

After talking for a few hours she stood and said, "I have a few errands to run." She took the elevator to the main floor and left the hospital. As she walked out into the sun she saw Dr. Wellington sitting at "their" bench," so she walked over and sat down with him. He raised his head from his book and smiled at her, "How are you today; pretty lady." She almost choked on that statement because she knew for sure she was not a pretty lady. "Thank you for the compliment, but I know I'm not that pretty." His mouth dropped because he knew she was a beauty right out of a picture book. "Faelynn, how can you think that? You look like a fashion model. Your face could grace the pages of any magazine and have half the country drooling over you." She really laughed then. She patted his arm, "Don't give me the big head, please." The doctor talked for a while about her grandmother. He explained how pleased he was at her progress.

Faelynn looked at him and frowned, "I'm not sure grandmother wanted us to go out together. She seemed a little disturbed about it. He thought about it for a minute. "Do you think it isn't proper for us to date?" She shrugged her shoulder then replied; "I think she is not used to us as dating. I explained it was just a charity event to help kids go to camp and she will be fine with it, perhaps she is afraid she will lose me again." She stood to leave and he stood with her. "I'll see you at around six thirty then." He stood looking into her face, "I'll be there with bells on." She laughed at his sudden humor. So underneath all that handsome man was a sense of humor and laughter, "Then don't ring them because you'll scare my neighbors to death. Remember they are all old." She walked to her car still smiling. She kept thinking how easy it was to like him and how well they got along together. They both seemed to be even tempered too.

She stopped for some milk and bread for her cereal and toast before going on to the house. She had a few hours and wanted to rest up some before tonight's dinner. She walked outside and cut a few of the lilacs off the bush to put them in a vase on the kitchen table. The fragrance filled the house giving off such a nice aroma.

She walked around to the back of the house to the shed to see what was stored there. When she opened it she saw just the tools to keep the yard clean. She went to the other shed and found boxes and plastic containers stored there.

She wondered what they were. She opened one of the plastic containers and looked at some of the papers. They were her father's things. She wondered why her grandmother had them stored here instead of in the basement of the house. There was plenty of room there because most of it was filled with wall shelving just for things like this. She picked up the container and carried it into the house. She placed the box on the desk so she could look through some of the papers to figure out just what they were and why they weren't in the basement. She stopped and took a deep breath and she could already smell the lilac's fragrance drifting through the house. She always loved flowers in the house.

She pulled out a few papers and began to read them. They were about her father's business, some accounting papers from his accountant. It looked like his business was doing well. It had a nice profit margin for sure.

She laid the paper aside and pulled out more of the papers and skimmed through them as she placed them in the other pile. She saw a bankbook ledger and opened it. It showed three accounts with substantial balances in them. She wondered if her grandmother had transferred the balances to another account.

She walked to the phone and called the Mr. Davis at the bank. When he got online she asked him about the accounts, "Could you please check this account and tell me if the money is still in it? She read the number to him and he came back to the phone. "Yes, Miss Myers the money is still in that account and it has grown quite a bit with the interest paid to in it the last fifteen years." She read him the other account numbers, "Yes, those funds are still there." She was in shock to know that her father still had open accounts at the bank for so long, "How can I get these funds transferred to my account. These accounts belonged to my father and my grandmother never moved them to the trust fund for me." Mr. Davis assured her, "Just bring me his death certificate and I can make the transfer then." She thanked him and hung up the phone.

She added the three accounts up and blew out her breath at the amount that had remained in the hidden accounts for all these years. She could go ahead and quit her job and live off this income for a while. Her father would have wanted her to have it. She closed the ledger and took it up to her room for safekeeping. Now, she had to find his death certificate. She didn't realize how much money her parents had actually had prior to their death. The only thing she had received was the trust fund from their insurance when they had died and she didn't want to touch that. She hadn't wanted to face the fact that they had died and she had gotten the settlement. She would have traded it any day to have them back with her. The money in the trust wasn't important to her as much as they had been.

She walked back downstairs to the container and continued to look through it. She found a few envelopes she opened and one was the death certificate for her father and the other was for her mother. She looked at her mothers and noticed the name of her parents. She laid those aside to take upstairs. She would like to look up some of her mother's relatives and she knew some still lived here. Her mother's parents had died before her mother had.

She wrote a quick note on her pad to check on that. She saw a book near the bottom of the plastic box and pulled it out to see what it was. It looked like she was going to have to visit that shed for some time to see what all was in there. Perhaps, her grandmother had been so distraught over losing her only son that she couldn't bear to deal with any of his business affairs. She was sure that had to be the reason. Perhaps when their home was cleaned out it was all stored in the most convenient place and she never had the desire to deal with it.

She looked at the front and back of the book but it gave no clue as to what was inside. She slowly opened the first page and read it. *This book belongs to Caroline Myers and is not to be read prior to her death.*

Faelynn held the book without breathing. She couldn't believe that she was going to read her mother's most secret thoughts and dreams. She trembled as she reached for up to turn the page. She stopped as she looked at some family history information on the front page. It had her grandparents name and their parents listed. It gave her mother's brothers and sisters names and their spouses. She had it all in her hands, her mother's most precious notes.

The phone rang but she was so absorbed she couldn't let go of the book to answer it. She looked up at the clock and realized that she had been looking in that box for hours. She closed the book and reached for the phone. "Hello." She heard nothing on the other end and hung the phone back into place. She had to hurry and get ready because Kurt would be there any minute to pick her up for the dinner-dance.

She rushed upstairs and into the shower. Spending the next few minutes getting dressed, fixing her hair and applying her makeup. She finished just as the doorbell rang. She walked down the stairs to see a very handsome man in a black tux standing at her door.

She opened it as she smiled up at him. He walked inside and handed her a lovely corsage for her dress. He helped pin it to the strap, "You look beautiful, I'm going to be the proudest man there escorting such a beautiful woman around tonight." She laughed because he had the ability to make her feel comfortable with him, "Or you could be the most unfortunate man to be stuck with me." He smiled but would never have agreed with her.

On the drive over to the dance she explained to Kurt, "I have found some of my parent's papers and a special book my mother wrote for me. I can hardly wait to get into the box tomorrow and see what else is there." Kurt looked at her, "I only wish I had parents who cared for me. I was raised in an orphanage and didn't know who my parents were. You're a lucky lady. In a way we're kind of like in the parents department. You lost yours before you really knew them and I didn't have any to begin with." She looked at him through sad eyes. How hard it must have been for him to struggle out of an orphanage to becoming a doctor. She admired him that much more. "You're right there. We have similar backgrounds. Neither of us had any love or parents to help us deal with growing up or learning to live in the world around us. The only thing pushing us was sheer desire to become something for ourselves. Most people don't realize how hard it was because they had people standing behind them supporting them." They looked at each other and he reached over and squeezed her hand. They had a bond because of it.

CHAPTER 6

The night was clear and fresh and excitement seemed to fill the air as they arrived at the country club. There were long lines of cars in front of them that were patiently waiting for the parking attendants to take their car and park it. It seemed that anyone who was anyone in town was at this dinner. She looked over at Kurt and stated, "You know this is the first time I have ever been to this place. I had lived here all my life and had never attended any of the functions here."

He couldn't believe that such a beautiful woman had missed all the gaiety and parties that Covington had to offer through all the organizations. But he never pursued the subject because he felt that she might not be comfortable talking about it. It had been a long time ago and he knew that her life then hadn't been that happy.

Their turn finally came and the doorman opened the door for Faelynn to get out. He held his hand to assist her. Kurt had walked around the car to take her arm and fold it into his. He smiled down at her with warm eyes, "Welcome to the ball, Cinderella. I hope I don't have to chase you down to give you back your glass slipper." He smiled and she followed suit.

She looked up into his laughing eyes, "Thank you for asking me." Then he heard his name and turned to see an elderly woman headed his way. He whispered to her, "Brace yourself for being introduced to a million people of whom you won't remember half of them." She looked at him and chuckled as she whispered back. "I'm ready Prince Charming." He patted her arm and met the woman head on.

The doctor stopped and shook hands with the woman in front of him. "Millie Ferguson, I'd like to present to you Miss Faelynn Myers." The ladies greeted each other and Millie inquired, "Are you perhaps related to Laura Myers? Faelynn watched the information flick over the woman's face, "Yes, she is my grandmother." She looked at Millie to see if there was any dislike in her eyes but saw none. Millie smiled as she said, "Please give her my best. I have missed working with her on different projects."

He excused them and walked further into the ballroom. "We should find a good tale before the best ones are gone." He settled on one near the patio doors so that they might slip out for air if they needed to.

They sat there looking around the room as other couples came into the room to find their tables. Soon everyone took their seat and the announcements began. Kurt noticed several people from the hospital that were there including one of the nurses from the fourth floor. She saw him looking at her and smiled to him. He smiled back and turned back to Faelynn. The speakers came and went as the program went on and on.

Soon the last speaker was there and announced that dinner was being served and the waiters would be bringing around the short menus for your choices so be ready to choose. Everyone laughed and the drove of waiters filled the room and each table was quickly dealt with. Kurt walked to the bar and ordered their drinks. Several men stopped him to talk about this or that but he went back to his table as quickly as possible.

The meal was delicious and both Kurt and Faelynn enjoyed it immensely. While they were enjoying their meal and talking, the waiters had cleared the center of the room of all the tables and chairs. The podium had been cleared also and there was a band sitting up as they watched. Faelynn turned to him, "You know Kurt, I haven't danced much and I'm not sure I can do the modern dances." He leaned close and whispered to her, "Don't worry, we'll only do the waltzes." She looked at him and smiled, "You must have read my mind." And they both laughed as they drank the champagne.

As she looked around the room again she noticed Richard standing at the doorway to the bar area. He was looking at her with a frown on his face. She turned her head quickly but not before Kurt had noticed the encounter. He sat his glass on the table, "Do you know Richard Helms?" She looked at him and let out a breath she had been holding, "Yes, we met during my senior year in school." Kurt said nothing more about Richard but did watch him now and then. Each time he seemed to be staring at Faelynn. The band had started playing some slow song and Kurt and Faelynn got up to dance. "Faelynn, don't let Richard's staring at you bother you. He's just jealous he didn't think to ask you himself." She smiled up at him not wanting to admit that Richard had asked her but she refused him, "I doubt he knew I was here until a few days ago. I don't get out much and I don't socialize with the community." He drew her closer to him and chuckled, "All the better for me then; no competition." They laughed as he swung her around at the end of the dance. He continued, "Did I tell you how beautiful you look in that outstanding dress. It is perfect for your blue eyes." She bent her head in a bow, "Thank you for noticing." He tucked her arm in his and looked into her beautiful eyes, as they walked to their table under the scrutinizing eyes of Mayer Helms.

Somehow Kurt enjoyed the Mayor of Covington following his every move especially knowing he coveted the beautiful woman who was his date. He chuckled to himself and thought of what their next conversation was going to be about. Richard Helms was a cool cookie, owner of carpentry and cabinet company, the hardware store and the Mayor of this town. But he wasn't very cool tonight he looked like he could spit nails especially at him.

He noticed she was a little flustered because of Richard's continuous staring at her so he suggested, "Would you like to take a break and get some fresh air on the veranda?" She nodded *yes* and they walked out through the patio doors. They stood there watching the moon reach the top of the sky and listened to the music drift out into the night. He took her hand and walked down the steps toward the large pond a few feet away. There were benches sat around the pond for people to rest and watch the vast amount of gold and exotic fish that were in it.

Just as they disappeared from sight, Richard had meandered over to the veranda. He cursed under his breath knowing that Faelynn was out with that wolf Wellington. No telling what he would talk her into. Women seem to flock to his feet, but he hoped Faelynn would have enough sense to see through him.

Kurt and Faelynn sat on the bench just listening to the night sounds. He held her hand for a long time before they went back inside. They sat at the table watching the activity in the room. There were several couples dancing around the room and Faelynn saw Richard dancing with a young woman she didn't know. She watched them until they came near the table then she dropped her eyes to look at her hands folded beneath the table.

Richard and the young woman looked good together dancing around in each other's arms. She chided herself; *stop thinking like that, he's not yours; never was and never will be.*

Richard had returned the lady to her table and was walking to Faelynn's table when he heard Wellington's beeper go off. He smiled as he arrived at the table. Kurt looked at his beeper and turned to Faelynn, "I have to get back to the hospital, would you like to leave now or stay a while and I'll make sure you get home."

Richard spoke up, "I'll be happy to see the young lady home Wellington. I know you have an emergency call to make." They both looked at Faelynn and she looked at both of them. Richard said, "Please stay Faelynn, I'll take you home when the dance is over." She wasn't sure she trusted him again but knew Kurt had to leave either way. "I'll be alright Kurt you go on to the hospital and take care of the problem there." At that same time the nurse that came with someone else was standing beside Richard, "Dr. Wellington, can I ride with you? I've been paged too. I can't imagine what it could be." Kurt looked at Faelynn again before leaving, "I'll call you tomorrow." She shook her head and he and the nurse left. Richard sat down beside her, "There is a slow dance coming up, may I have this dance?" She looked at him wondering why she had agreed to stay and let him take her home, "Didn't you come to the dance with anyone or do you always expect to pick someone up?" He looked at how beautiful she looked, "No, I didn't invite anyone to come to the dance with me because I'm not dating. I have a daughter to care for, so I don't have much time for myself or too many other people.

She looked surprise at his announcement, "You have a daughter?" He smiled at her and beamed with pride thinking of his little angel, "Yes, she is a beautiful little girl named Alexandria. She is four years old and is worshipped by her daddy." Faelynn was curious now about his wife and daughter, "Where is her mother?" He looked uncomfortable with her question, perhaps she shouldn't have asked; "She passed away two years ago on a motorcycle accident when the man she was riding with went off a cliff." Faelynn wrinkled her brow, "I'm very sorry. I didn't know you had even gotten married but I assumed you probably would have."

The music started to play again and it was a beautiful love Ballard. He turned and looked at her, "This is the slow song I asked them to play for us. Do you remember it?" He took her hand and led her to the floor and enfolded her into his arms. She smelled so sweet and she felt so right in his arms. He held her so close so that she couldn't get away from him again.

He wondered if she ever knew how much he loved her. How much he wanted to spend the rest of his life with her? How he had hurt after she had cut him out of her life? She wouldn't even let him explain. But he continued to love her. She was his first and only love.

The woman he married in name only so that the child she was having would legally have his name, meant nothing to him. They never lived together or slept together it was a debt paid to an old friend.

She had needed his help and he had wanted her child. It belonged to a high school buddy of his that had no family and he had promised to take care of his daughter on his deathbed and he has been doing that. He loved Alexandria as much as if she were his that is because now she was.

Richard almost forgot anyone else was in the room with them. She had to whisper into his ear, "The music has stopped." He looked down at her with chagrin and smiled, "I knew that and laughed." He took her hand and they walked out onto the veranda for some fresh air. They stopped at the far end of the large porch and he turned and asked, "Would you like to go on a picnic tomorrow?"

She surprised herself by accepting, "Yes, where are you taking me?" He ran his finger down her cheek, "To the lake. But don't tell anyone it's a secret." She laughed and put her hand on his arm, "I won't, what time are you picking me up?" He thought for a minute before responding, "How about ten in the morning and we can spend a few hours at the lake." She nodded, *yes*, but then looked at her watch, "It's getting late and I need to get home. I have been working on some plans for the house I need to finish this weekend."

He drove her home and walked her to the door. He waited while she opened the door and walked into the house to the back door to check it. It seemed tight and no one had tried to get inside. There didn't seem to be any disturbance in the house. He walked back to the front door, "Everything looks good and nothing is out of place. I'd better be getting on home to check on Alexandria. I'll see you tomorrow at ten then. Wear something comfortable and some sandals." He pulled her into his arms and gave her a quick warm kiss then released her before she could object.

He told her to lock the door when he stepped outside, which she promptly did. He waved and went out to his car and drove away. He seemed happy they were able to talk now, instead of the cold shoulder she had given him before when he had tried to talk to her about what happened between them.

She walked into her living room and sat down to think. *Just how bad did she want to have a relationship with Richard? He had treated her so badly when he took her to the prom. Could she ever forgive him for that? Why did he want to see her now? What had changed other than he had gotten married and she hadn't?* There were a lot of changes going on in her life now.

She needed to move slow and easy with all of them. She needed a priority list and at the top of it she would put Michael. She needed to let him know she wasn't interested in getting married to him. There was no sense in having him hold onto the hope of her marrying him because she hadn't wanted it a month ago and still didn't want it now. She checked the clock. It was ten o'clock here so it would be seven o'clock there. She could call him now and get it over with before she got cold feet.

She picked up the phone and dialed his number in Portland. The phone rang several times but he didn't pick it up. His answering machine came on and she left a message for him to return her call when he got in. There that was one thing that was in the works. Now she needed to know what she was going to say to try to be as gentle as possible. But it had to be the truth too. She walked up the stairs to change into her nightgown. She came back down to the kitchen to make herself a cup of tea. She took it into the study where she had left the box of papers that belonged to her father.

She started to look into the plastic container again while waiting for Michael to call. She lifted out more papers and went through them as she sorted the important must read ones and the not so important ones she could read later. She found a bundle of papers tied in a bow. She untied them and saw what looked like real estate records. She read them and reread them.

It was about her parent's home. It was at 2942 Sycamore Street just a few streets over. Her grandmother had the documents to the house but there was no record of sale. She wondered if her grandmother had sold it or did she keep it like the business accounts of her fathers. She would walk over there tomorrow to look at the house. She couldn't even remember what it would have looked like. Why had her grandmother not given her these when she turned eighteen? She thought of her having suffered through losing her only son. It was as bad as her having lost both parents.

She sat the papers in the important stack and pulled more out of the container. There was another bundle of papers near the bottom of the container wrapped in pink ribbon. She pulled the ribbon open and unfolded the papers. They were official court papers. She couldn't imagine what they were about until she started reading the first few pages. It mentioned her name and her parents name and a birth certificate with the word adoption written on it.

She stopped and looked at the paper again. Adopted, she was adopted, but how could that be. Her parents had loved her so much. Why didn't they tell her she was adopted? Why hadn't her grandmother told her she was adopted? She sat there as many things drifted through her head. Was that why her grandmother didn't love her because she was adopted? She was not truly her granddaughter. Was that why her grandmother rejected her when she came to live with her? Yet, no one felt she had the need to know.

This would surely explain why her grandmother had acted so cold to her as a child, but what a bitter way to act toward a child who didn't know she was adopted. Could she ever forgive them for keeping this from her? But her mother had loved her more than anything. Her father had doted on her and treated her like she was the love of his life. Her grandmother who treated her like a stranger in her home, one that she lived for many years without the warmth of family. She couldn't hold back the tears and they streamed down her cheeks as fast as a river flowed. Tears, she had been holding back had dammed them up inside her promising not to ever cry or ask for love.

She put her hands over her face and let them flow, for the loss of her beloved mother and father. For the love that had been lost between granddaughter and grandmother for the love of a partner that she had turned away from because she couldn't believe it was real love. All lost for nothing. For all the pain that they had endured because of the misunderstanding cost them dearly. She placed the letters in the folder and placed them in the important file. She pulled another bundle of paper out wrapped in blue.

They looked the same as her adoption papers. Did they have a boy child somewhere? Her hands shook as she untied the blue ribbon. There were more court papers for a little boy named Mark Anthony Hollister. He was two years old and his mother was an unwed mother that lived in Alabama. They were going to take possession of this young man when they returned from their honeymoon trip to Europe. She clutched the papers to her chest and thought to herself, oh Mark Anthony what happened to you? Where are you now? And can I find you? Yes, she shouted Yes, I can find him I will find him.

She placed those papers into her important stack. She found the bottom of the container and pulled out all of the remaining papers and began to read them. It was her parent's will. She laid it on the desk and walked to the kitchen to make herself another cup of tea. She walked back into the small office-den and picked up the will again and began to read. Her mother and father both had wills clipped together. She read her fathers and it had left everything to her mother and her. She read her mother's and it had left everything to her. It did list several specific pieces of things that she wanted her to have. She read the list and had no idea where they were or who had them. She would have to ask her grandmother where these things were. She looked up from the desk and realized that she would also have to tell her grandmother that she had found the box and looked at all the papers in it. She thought for a long time on the consequences of opening the box and mentioning it to her grandmother. What a Pandora's Box it could be for them both.

In one way it could bond them together but in another it could tear them apart. What would be best for them both? This is going to be one of her hardest decisions that she has ever had to make.

It was well after midnight and still there was no call from Michael. She had hoped to talk to him to clear the air for both of them. Then her next step would be to go to Oregon to resign her position and clear out her apartment. The closer the time came for her to do that the more she was ready to get it done with. Her job and her boss had been good to her over the years but now it was time to make a move and it needed to be done swiftly and quickly.

She would talk to her grandmother tomorrow to let her know she was flying back to Oregon to pack her things and resign her job. It wouldn't take more than a week to be finished with her current life as she had known it. That was a thought provoking moment. The entire life she had built for herself in Oregon vanished in a week's time. Did she have any regrets? Some, yes, there were some, but not to the point of remaining there. She had enjoyed her lifestyle, the freedom, and her few friends.

She packed the important papers back in the plastic container and snapped the lid shut. The non-important papers she stacked them on the desk and sat looking at them one by one. She found one of her shoeboxes when she went upstairs and brought it back to stack the papers in it.

The first report was on her father's business. She read it completely through. It sounded like her father had many investments that he had dabbled in while in business. She had circled the information on the report so that she could contact the firms to see if her father still had stocks and bonds there. She went through the other papers and discovered quite a portfolio of investments. Perhaps she should consult an attorney and let him handle it. It was quite extensive and mind boggling to her.

She looked at her clock again and it was after two in the morning. She picked up the phone and dialed Michael's number again. Still no answer, she left a second message for a call back. She yawned and decided it was time of her to go to bed and she cut off all the lights and went upstairs.

The phone rang around four in the morning and she thought perhaps it was Michael coming home from some event he had attended. She answered it, "Hello." Michael was on the line, "Hello, Faelynn, I got your messages and am returning your call." She thought it best not to tell him over the phone but instead see him while she was in Oregon next week. She replied, "Michael, I am flying home next week and would like to have dinner with you if you can make the time." Michael sounded a little strange but said, "Of course, it will be nice to see you again. I have missed you." She thought something sounded funny in his voice kind of distant, "Okay, I should be there on Tuesday, so how about Tuesday night at O'Brien's. I can meet you there around six is that good for you? I want to stop and see Annie and Phyllis too. I have missed everyone."

Michael replied, "Yes, that will be fine and I can't wait to see you, it's been too long." She told him it was very early in the morning and she had to go back to the hospital that morning so they both said their goodbyes and hung up the phone. Something kept eating at her trying to figure out what was the matter with Michael. He acted and sounded so odd compared to his normal actions. She put her head back down on the pillow and had drifted off to sleep in no time.

She had set her alarm to wake her up early so she could visit with her grandmother for an hour before Richard was to come over. She showered and went down stairs to get her coffee, cereal and toast. She walked back into the small den and slid the boxes she had looked through under a cabinet out of the way. She dragged a chair in front of them so that no one would notice if they had walked into the office. She was not sure why she did that but it made her feel better.

She picked up her purse and walked out the door to her car. She drove to the hospital very early so she could talk to her grandmother. When she got there she met the doctor again at their bench. "I am leaving Monday for Portland. I've decided to go ahead and resign my job and pack my things to have them shipped here. I have something personal I have to do there too." He listened intently then looked into her eyes, "How long will you be gone?" She looked at her hands folded tightly in her lap, "Possibly a week. I'm going to talk to grandmother this morning so I can make sure she understands I will be back."

Kurt looked at her as she was organizing her priorities for this trip, "Faelynn, what is the personal thing you have to take care of?" She thought for a minute and wasn't sure she wanted to share that with him; after all it was not any of his business. It was something that happened prior to meeting him. She looked at him and said, "Kurt, I know there are things in your life that you wouldn't want to share with me, especially since we have just met. I am just not ready to talk about that part of my life right now, with you or anyone else. I hope you can allow me my privacy right now. Perhaps, someday I can share it, but not yet.' He reached over and put his hand over hers, "I understand. I wish you a speedy return." They stood and he walked to his car and she went into the hospital.

She turned to watch him pull out of the parking lot then turned toward the elevator. She walked into her grandmother's room and saw she was eating her breakfast. She took her seat beside the bed and watched her with a smile. "My, that must be good. I haven't seen you eat like this in a while." Her grandmother smiled and sipped her coffee; "I need to get my strength back so I can race you up and down the stairs". They both laughed.

Her grandmother could see the troubled look on her face but didn't ask what put it there, "Is there a problem I can help you with Faelynn? If I can, you know I will do anything for you." She smiled at her grandmother and patted her on the arm. "Grandmother, I have to make a trip back to Portland to clear up some things there and I need to be gone for almost a week. I wonder if you can stay strong for me. Continue to work on your exercises and keep getting better, so that when I return you can come home to live.

Can you be strong for me while I am gone? I've tried to think of any other way to do this and be professional about it and there is no other way than to do it but in person. The Webb firm has been very good to me and I owe them this. I have written my letter of resignation and when I deliver it, I will have all my things pack and shipped so that when I get back they will have already arrived at the house."

Her grandmother took her hand in hers and squeezed it gently, "Faelynn, I am so happy to have you move back with me. I know you have built a life there for yourself but you're needed here so badly. I want our relationship to grow closer.

I was a fool when you came to live with me for putting those frivolous hens before you but I am much wiser and know that our family, you and me, come before anyone else. Go and get your affairs taken care of. I'll be waiting here for you when you return.

Faelynn hugged her tightly, "I just wanted you to be comfortable with my leaving and knowing that I will be returning as soon as possible." Faelynn kissed her on the cheek. She did add something else. "I will be leaving early Monday morning. I intend to go to my apartment and pack the entire day Monday and on Tuesday I will call an express shipping firm to pick them up for me. It might take a day or two for them to pick up so I will have to play that by ear. On Tuesday I will go to the firm and speak with my boss and Tuesday night I will say good bye to the friends I met there I will probably have to stay over until Wednesday or Thursday to get everything settled with the job as I have some papers to sign and some accounts to change.

I am hoping to be back by Friday morning at the latest. I'll be back tomorrow for a while but I need to figure out what I'm taking with me. It won't be much as there isn't much sense in taking it and bringing it back. I will most likely take an overnight case. Oh, having to figure all this out gives me a headache." She laughed and so did her grandmother. "Soon, it will be all done and you can rest," her grandmother assured her. "Yes, that is true. I can rest and relax for a while. Maybe we can put in a garden and make the yard as pretty as it used to be?" Her grandmother yawned unable to hide how tired she was from her last walk, "Yes, it would be nice to see the yard as beautiful as it used to be. She drifted off to sleep. Faelynn covered her with the light spread and kissed her cheek once more before she tip toed out the door.

She made it back home just in time to see Richard and his daughter pull into her driveway. She waved at them and rushed into the house to change into her sweats and get a sweater from her closet. When she came back down she went to the kitchen to get a bottle of water and saw that someone had been in the house. She walked to the door and motioned for Richard to come inside. When he got to the door he saw the frightened look on her face. He put his arm around her and whispered, "What is it?" She looked so frightened and kept looking back toward the kitchen, "Someone's been in the house." He motioned for her to call the police with his hand to his ear. She understood and he put his daughter's hand in hers and when they went into the living room he closed the door behind them. He looked around for some weapon if he should need it and found an old baseball bat in the umbrella rack.

He picked it up and walked toward the kitchen. He heard a noise in the little room off of the kitchen. He walked to the door as quietly as possible and peeked inside to see a man leaning over the desk riffling through all the drawers. He knew who it was right away. It was Steven Smith. He must have gotten out of jail and came back to terrorize Faelynn.

He spoke to the man and he jumped and started to run at him, yelling at a full run. Richard stepped back and raised the bat and as he came through the door; he swung it and caught him in the chest, knocking the wind out of him. In the distance, he heard the siren of the police car. It stopped outside and two officers rushed into the house.

Richard explained to them what had happened and they called the ambulance for the man lying on the ground. Richard handed them the bat, "Faelynn is in the living room with my daughter. I'd like to take her out of here before anyone else gets here." They agreed and he went to get his daughter.

He kissed Faelynn and squeezed her arm gently, "I'll be right back I want to take her back home for an hour or so. I don't want her upset at seeing the police here." Faelynn agreed and he left with his daughter. He returned in a few minutes and stayed with her through the whole ordeal. The police arrested him and promised that he wouldn't be out again. She wasn't sure she believed them this time. If he got out once he could do it again. How safe will she be as long as he is alive? She hoped this time the courts would see how dangerous he is and that he could have killed her had she not heard him before hand.

CHAPTER 7

Richard sent his crew back to her house to fix her back door again. She had an errand to run early that morning. She had called the airline for a return trip to Oregon for late Monday and that gave her some time to get a few things done. She had looked into the office and was so glad that she had hid the paperwork behind the chair and Steven hadn't found it. He would have used it to embarrass or humiliate her within the community.

She had taken her mother and father's death certificates to the bank and had Mr. Davis close the accounts and transfer them into her trust fund. With the interest added to the regular balance it made a tidy fund of over a million dollars into her account. Fifteen years is a long time to draw interest on that large of money. She went to an attorney referred to her by Mr. Davis and spoke with him about finding the young man that was supposed to have been her brother.

She gave Mr. Robinson copies of all the adoption papers and asked that he hire a detective to find him. But she didn't want him to be told who was looking for him. She wanted to meet him first to see what he would have been like. She wanted to know if anyone had told him that he was to be adopted. That would have to wait until she returned.

The other thing she wanted to talk to him about was the stocks and bonds that her parents had invested in through the business. He said he would check into it and when she returned they could discuss it. She signed papers for him to work on her cases and gave him a check for his services. He gave her receipts for the things she had hired him to do.

She walked out of the office with a load of worry taken off her shoulders. She checked three more things off her list of things to do. There was one more thing for her to do before boarding the plane for Portland. She got in her car and drove to Sycamore Street and pulled along the curb. She got out and walked with the piece of paper in her hand. She found the address in no time and stood outside the home looking at it.

She remembered what it had looked like but was too young to remember her address. She walked into the yard to look closer and it looked empty. Had her grandmother kept it all these years without selling it? She looked into the back yard and there was a swing set and a few bouncing animals that were mounted into the ground. She peeked into the house and there was all her parents' furniture as she remembered it. It looked as if it had sat there waiting for her. But where was the key. She looked on her grandmother's key chain and tried one of the keys; she didn't know what it went to. It fit and the door clicked open.

She went inside and looked from room to room all her memories came flooding back to her. There were all the things she remembered sitting right out on the tables. She walked to her room and it looked exactly as she had walked out of it so many years ago.

This was her home and she knew it. She walked into her mother and father's room and it looked exactly the same. She looked into the jewelry box that sat on the dresser and was surprised to see all her jewelry still inside. Even some of the pieces she had mentioned in her will. These were worth a fortune now. She should take them to the bank and put in a safety box. They were much too valuable to leave in an empty house. She picked it up and walked back to the living room. She looked into the kitchen and the dining room and the beautiful antique dishes that rested in the china closet.

Time was slipping away and she had to leave. She took the jewelry box and drove right to the bank. She opened a safety deposit box and put the entire box inside. She took her key and added it to her new set of keys she was putting together.

She stopped by the hospital for a minute to say good-bye to her grandmother before leaving. She found the room empty and asked at the nurse's station where she could be found. They all replied Dr. Wellington took her to the cafeteria for dinner. There was so much envy in their statement they blushed. Faelynn laughed on the way back to the cafeteria where she found Dr. Wellington and her grandmother laughing and talking. She joined them and ordered a sandwich and a glass of tea. She enjoyed the meal and the company and hugged them both before leaving for the airport. She would leave the car there until she returned. She thought it was wonderful that her grandmother had such a good friend in her doctor. She boarded the plane with only her overnight bag and took her seat to read some more of her mother's book. This was the perfect time to read this very personal and private book.

The night dragged on as the hours passed taking her closer to the end of her life as she knew it for the last six years. She was now ready to face the future and her future was going to be in Covington Georgia. She arrived early Tuesday morning and went to her apartment to pack. She had gotten some boxes from the company who would be moving her, when she was finished. She stacked and packed boxes with all her personal things. She had a chance to look around her small apartment and noticed how sparse it was and wondered why had she hadn't noticed it before. She lived in an apartment with just a few pieces of furniture and very little else. There were a few pictures, a few dishes, hardly anything that she could have called a home.

She measured how much she had gotten done and how much longer it would take her to finish packing. It seemed funny to her that her six years of her life was all packed and ready to move. She looked at her watch and realized it had been hours since she had eaten. She went to her kitchen to see what she could fix quickly and clean her refrigerator out at the same time. She opened a can of soup and found some crackers, hoping they weren't too old to eat. While sitting at her table she found her notepad and pen, she started jotting down things she needed to check before leaving. The first thing she would be doing is to go see Mr. Webb and resign from her job, then she would start working down her list of things to do, such as making sure the everything was closed or stopped and her new address given to them for her refund.

She needed to put in a change of address at the post office. Close her checking account at the bank. Call the express company to pick up her boxes for shipping and meet her friends at O'Brien's that night. Then she could get back on a plane for home. She quickly disposed of the things in her refrigerator and packed up her meager can goods to drop off at a charity or soup kitchen.

She walked into the bedroom to make sure it was finished then walked back to the living room and finished taping all the boxes and marking them with her grandmother's address. She called the express company and they would be there in an hour, what luck, she thought she might have to wait a day or so to get them to pick up her boxes. She left her apartment and walked to the bank down the street. She met with a loan officer and had her account cleaned out and closed. She stopped at the post office and had the change of address done. Three things marked off her lists that were done quickly. She walked to the job she had found after moving here. When she reached the tenth floor she disembarked the elevator. She walked directly to her boss's office so she could get this over quickly. She stopped at his secretary's desk and asked to see him. She sat and waited for a few minutes before he came to the door and invited her inside.

He shook hands with her and asked if her grandmother was up and about. "Faelynn, it's nice to see you back. We've missed you and many of your clients have asked about you." She smiled and sat in the chair before his desk. Her boss watched her as she sat there quietly. She spoke to him in a very soft low tone. "Mr. Webb, I've had to face some very hard things in my life when I went back home to care for my grandmother. She desperately needs me now and so I must resign my position here to take care of her. She reached into her purse and handed him an envelope with her typed resignation inside. He reached to take it, "Faelynn is this really what you want to do. I know when you first hired in here that you wanted to escape from her and build your own life." She smiled at him knowing that was exactly what she had wanted to do, "Yes, that is what I wanted back then but now after seeing her and being with her we are rebuilding the gap between us and she can no longer live alone. She is fragile and needs me badly. I can't let her down this time. Mr. Webb, I want you to know how much I appreciated your giving me this job and the opportunity to expand and grow in your company. You allowed me to follow my own direction and become who I am today. I will always be grateful to you for doing that, but after much soul searching I find that I must go back and now is the right time. I have thoroughly enjoyed working for you and will never forget my experiences here."

She stood to leave but he walked around his desk to stand in front of her, "Faelynn, if you ever need a job or I can help you in any way, don't hesitate to contact me. You have been an excellent employee and I shall miss you very much but I do understand some of your personal life and I can only say, we will miss you very much and please send us a note now and then. Who knows I might open an office in Atlanta to entice you back into my service." He enfolded her into his arms because she had become like his child because he had watched over her as he whispered, "Always remember family comes first, good luck to you and God Bless."

She nodded her head as she walked out to her office to clean it out. She had put two boxes in it earlier. She took her personal pictures and things that she had brought with her and a small plant. She took the plant and dropped it off in the lounge hoping someone would take it. She met several of her co-workers who were there on break, "I have enjoyed working with you all and will miss you." She turned and walked out of the office before anyone could say anything.

She walked back to her apartment and boxed the last bit of stuff into one box and taped and labeled it for shipping. She stopped to look around her just as the doorbell rang. She opened it to find the express driver with a furniture mover in his hand. He started putting the boxes on the mover and took the two loads down to his truck and came back to give her a receipt which she tucked into her purse.

She had already written to the apartment complex giving them her notice so that had all been taken care of. Her return plane ticket and the money from her checking account were in her purse too. She looked around her cleaned and now empty apartment and sighed. She was almost done. She was meeting Michael in one hour and her two friends would join them a half hour later. Then she would make her plane at ten and be off again.

Things were going much better than planned. She had gotten all the things on her list done and was walking toward O'Brien's to meet Michael. She stood in the doorway and looked for him in their regular place. They would meet there on Friday's after work for the happy hour treats then she wouldn't have to cook for herself that night.

She saw him sitting there drinking his beer. He hadn't noticed her so she walked over to the table and stood beside him. He stood up and gave her a hug. He held her chair for her to sit down. He looked at her for some time before speaking, "Welcome back to Oregon, Faelynn." She noticed that he didn't seem to be as enthusiastic as he normally was and wondered what brought on this subdued tone. She smiled at him knowing this would be their last meeting, "Thank you, Michael, but I'm not here to stay." His eyes wondered over her again, "How long are you staying?" Faelynn was surprised at his tone of voice almost as if he couldn't wait to get rid of her. She smiled at him hoping to ease some of his anxiety, "Shortly, then I will be on a plane back to Georgia." He looked confused and waited for her to continue. "Michael, I know that this is short notice but I've resigned my position at Webb Marketing Incorporated and have decided to move back to Georgia. My grandmother is having a hard time and healing is coming along slowly. I've decided the best thing for her and me is if I move back and take care of her. She is up in age and there is no one else but the two of us."

Michael almost smiled but withheld it. "I'm sorry to see you go Faelynn. I had thought once you were back that we could make our relationship more permanent." She looked at him and saw the burden had lifted from him and knew that he had changed his mind about proposing to her. She felt that it would be better to keep it light and as old friends instead of the troubled let down she had thought to be coming.

"So Michael, what have you been up to and how is life treating you and how is your job coming along?" With a barrage of questions he smiled because he knew she knew already. What a dear person she was to make light of it for him. "Oh, it is the same old job and the same old company. I started dropping by another hangout on Friday's for happy hour. It is closer to my apartment and I met some really nice people there. I haven't been in here since you left." She patted his arm and replied, "That is great Michael; I'll miss our happy hours when I leave." He turned his glass in his hand then looked at her, "So when are you leaving, Faelynn?"

She looked at her watch, "I have to catch a flight in one hour. I hope you don't mind but I invited Phyllis and Annie to drop by so that I could say goodbye to them also. I'm really on a tight schedule but I didn't want to miss the three of you, my best friends." Michael smiled and put his hand to her cheek. "You always were such a special person. I'm proud to have known you and wish you much happiness. Perhaps, when I'm in Georgia, I can call you and we can meet somewhere for lunch."

She touched his hand and smiled into his gentle face, "That would be lovely and yes, please do call me if you get out that way, I'd love to meet you for lunch or drinks." About that time two noisy women swept through the door calling her name. Michael couldn't help but laugh as she jumped up and ran to hug them both. They were jumping around and squealing you would have thought they hadn't seen each other in years.

They eventually drifted back over to the table and all three sat down with Michael. Greetings went around the table as Michael ordered them drinks.

They chatted for another twenty minutes before Michael stood up and she knew it was the last goodbye, "Well, Faelynn, I have to be on my way. I'm meeting someone for happy hour and I want to be on time." She beamed at him and stood to give him a big hug and a kiss on the cheek. "I'll miss you Michael and wish you the very best of luck and much happiness." He held her close and whispered, "I wish the same to you my friend." She smiled up at him and he kissed her on the cheek, then he turned to walk out the door. She rejoined the girls and they looked at her and Annie asked, "What was that all about?" She smiled as she watched him cross the street to his car, "I think Michael has found the right girl finally." They all held up their glasses for a toast to Michael and his happiness. They shared snack food and a drink through some very good conversation but the time went fast and Faelynn had to catch a plane. She hugged the girls and told them to be sure to stop by and see her or take their vacations and spend it with her. They both promised somehow, they would be visiting with her.

She had the bartender call a cab for her and she picked up her overnight bag from behind the counter then they walked outside as it arrived. She hugged the girls once again before getting into the cab. They were still waving as it drove away. She made her flight on time and as the plane took off from the runway she leaned her head back on the seat to rest for a while. Her thoughts drifted back to how smooth this return trip had been. No problems no hurt feelings, just good friends saying their goodbyes and moving on to another place and time.

She drifted off to sleep thinking of her good friends and how she'll miss them. She woke with a start as she heard the engines revved. She looked out the window but it was still dark. She wondered where they were at and what airport they were stopping at. The intercom came on and then the stewardess spoke to the passengers. "Could I have your attention please? The plane will be landing in Albuquerque New Mexico for an unexpected stop. We have a soon to be mother with unexpected complications that will need the assistance of a doctor during her delivery. We will just be stopping to let the couple off and then we will be airborne again. Thank you for being so patience. Congratulations to the soon to be new parents.

Everyone smiled, as paramedics assisted the very pregnant, young mother off the plane with the anxious young father following close behind. The plane taxied off the runway again and was in flight in no time. Faelynn laid her head back to rest again but didn't go back to sleep. This time she thought of her future and what it held. She thought of what she wanted from life and how she wanted to live it to make her happy. She also thought of her Pandora's Box and what to do about it.

She was definitely going to be throwing herself into some work projects that would keep her busy for some time. Painting the house inside and out and major remodeling will have to be done in her old room. Then there was her parent's home. She wanted to go through it and remove some of the valuable stuff still sitting in it. She didn't think she could sell it or rent it so that was something that needed to be decided. Why her grandmother had just locked everything up and left it as it was baffled her. She didn't know why, she chose to leave it, as it was, but she was very happy she had.

Then she thought of the lawyer she had hired. She needed to see him right away to see how the progress was coming on finding her brother. A brother, she had a brother. She was so happy that she had discovered that. What would he be like, how did he grow up? She was anxious to get busy now on getting her personal life back in order.

The plane descended toward the Atlanta airport as the sky broke daylight. She was tired and in need of a shower. She would go see her grandmother after she had a brief nap and freshened up. The passengers were walking into the airport when someone called to her. She looked up to see Richard and his little girl waiting for her. She smiled at them but was enfolded into his arms before she could protest. She stammered as she looked from one to the other, "What are you doing here? How did you know when I'd be here?" He looked at her and laughed, "Do you think I'd miss your homecoming?" He picked up his little girl and thrust the child toward her, "Alexandria give our homecoming girl a hug."

The little girl's chubby arms reached for her and she bent to welcome the hug. She kissed her on the cheek, "Thank you for that warm welcome Alexandria." She looked back at Richard and he had a big smile on his face. "Welcome back Faelynn," And he kissed her too, but not on the cheek. She blushed when he released her and bent to pick up her bag.

They walked to his car as he strapped his daughter into the baby seat, she settled herself into the front seat. They talked on the ride to her home about how things had gone while she was away. She felt such relief to have it over and done, "I got done sooner than expected and was glad to get a connecting flight out. It's funny how everything fell in to place for me when I arrived there." He took a quick glimpse to see if she really was happy it was done and over with, "Are you glad it's done or will you always wonder if you did the right thing?"

She returned his smile completely satisfied, "No, I know I did the right thing this time." He reached over and squeezed her hand. "I, for one am very glad it is over and you're back where you belong." The little bright-eyed girl in the back seat yelled out, "Daddy, are we going to get some ice cream now? You said if I was a good girl I could have ice cream?' Richard and Faelynn both laughed, "You had to bribe her?" He shook his head yes, and they laughed again.

He stopped at a red light and looked at her, "Someday, I'd like to tell you the story about her." She checked on the little girl in the back seat. "Someday, I'd like to hear it and might even add a story of my own." He gave her a funny look then returned to watching traffic and his driving.

He helped her with her case once they arrived at her home. It looked the same but she did ask him, "Were you able to get the back door fixed after Steven Smith broke into it again." He looked at her and replied, "Put your bag inside and step out back with me." She did as he asked and as they walked around to the back yard she looked at the newly done door. "Oh my, that looks absolutely beautiful." She could hardly believe her eyes. The new steel door now held a fairly large black security door too. She laughed and said, "It will take him all night to get into that if he tries it again." Richard stood looking at her for a few minutes. "If you want one on the front door it can be installed tomorrow. I already ordered it."

She looked at him in surprise. "Do you think I should have one?" He didn't hesitate with his answer, "Absolutely, there is never enough security to protect our loved ones." His little girl stood quietly holding her daddy's had as they talked. She looked up at both of them, "Daddy, do I get my ice cream now?" They both laughed. Richard replied, "In a few minutes. She has a one track mind when it comes to ice cream."

Faelynn looked at her and him and whispered, "I have some in my freezer if you'd like to stay and have a dish." He smiled then winked at her, "We, Helms never turn down a dish of ice cream. Do we sweetheart?" His daughter shook her head and looked at Faelynn waiting patiently for her ice cream. They walked around front and into the house to the kitchen table. She got the dishes and spoons and went to the freezer for the tube of vanilla ice cream. Richard dipped it into the dishes and they sat there peacefully eating the delicious cold treat.

Faelynn knew she had a lot to do today. Richard watched her thoughts drift of occasionally, "Look, I know you're going to be busy for a while, I'll take Alexandria home and see you later today, sometime. Faelynn agreed and they walked down the steps and out to his car. She waved as he drove out of her yard. She put the dishes into the sink just as the phone rang.

She picked it up and said, "Hello." The voice on the other end belonged to Dr. Wellington. "Hello, I was just checking to see if you had gotten home alright and how things went in Oregon." She smiled as she said back to him, "Everything actually went good and I got everything accomplished in one trip. I should be down to the hospital in an hour or so maybe, we can have coffee when I get there and talk for a few minutes." He seemed pleased with that and they said goodbye and hung up the phone.

She went upstairs to take a quick shower and change clothes. She had slept in the ones she had on while waiting for the plane to get to Atlanta. She made her way back to the attorney's office to see what progress he had made. She was ushered right into his office even though there was a room full of clients in his lobby.

She sat in front of his desk, as she waited for his report. He pulled the folder from his bottom drawer and hit his buzzer for his secretary. He told her to bring some coffee for both of them. Faelynn looked puzzled and wondered why he had done that? He waited until his secretary arrived with the coffee and sat one cup in front of each of them before he began. She picked up her cup to take a sip as she listened to him read to her.

Her mind whizzed by most of what he said, but then it said, wait what? What was he saying? The cup shook in her hand as she tried to put it down on the desk. He stopped to watch her. He asked, "Did you understand any of what I told you?" Her eyes were as big as saucers as she shook her head, *no*.

He got up from his chair and walked around to sit next to her. He gave her the report to read for herself. He went over some of it verbally as her eyes focused on the paper. "Faelynn, you are a very wealthy woman. Your father's investments were far more than what you brought me to look at, when I contacted some of the companies that he had stocks and bonds in they gave me other businesses that he either owned or had money invested in them." Your father was a financial genius when it came to investing.

He got up and walked back around his desk and sat down. She stood up to leave but he said, "Wait there is one more thing." He picked up the last page of the report and said, "We aren't quite through with collecting information but right now Faelynn it looks like your investment portfolio is probably worth between five to ten million dollars and that is just an estimated guess. He looked up to see Faelynn's reaction and she was not there. He looked over his desk and she lay crumpled on the floor. He buzzed for his secretary again and in an urgent manner. She brought the smelling salts and a wet cloth for her head. His secretary revived her enough to get her back into the chair. The lawyer looked at this normally composed woman, "Are you going to be able to drive yourself home?" She heard him but hadn't understood it all yet. "If you have an empty office, I would like to sit down and recover for a minute or two." Before she went into the other office he added one other thing. "Oh, and about the adopted brother, I haven't found him yet, but I will soon and then you can be reunited."

She thanked him and slipped into the other office to sit down and think about all this. She repeated all that he had told her of her father's investments. Her hands still shook as she reread the papers he had given her. She tried to comprehend all the wealth that she had discovered but it was very hard to digest. She needed to make sure she had calmed down because her next stop would be the hospital. She was sure that her grandmother hadn't had a clue about the investments.

She felt more stable and slipped out the door and waved at the receptionist on her way out. She drove to the hospital to see her grandmother. When she arrived there, Dr. Wellington was waiting on her outside on their bench. She laughed and thought she was going to have their name engraved on that bench. They had talked so many problems out that it would be well worth it. She walked up and sat down as he gave her a quick hug. "I'm so glad your home. You're grandmother has really missed you even though it has only been a few days. By the way so have I." They laughed together before she voiced her concern, "How is grandmother? Is she still chasing the doctors up and down the hall? I hope she is just about ready to come home because hospital food is getting old." He looked at her face, as it seemed to glow, "Is that a hint that I should take you to dinner tonight?" She laughed and pleaded off as she explained, "I have been on a long and tiring journey and I would just like to sleep off the jet lag for a day or two."

He agreed but did tell her something of interest. "Your grandmother is doing great and I think in a day or two she could come home. But only if you have some help to wait on her. It can be tiring to wait on someone by yourself without a break. It's not healthy for you or her because she will become more dependent and want you to wait on her hand and foot. You need someone to come in at least ten to twelve hours a day. There are no diversions from that schedule and I mean it. You are not to run yourself down waiting on her. She needs to learn to wait on herself again. Are we agreed?" Faelynn knew he was right. She would need a break from the house during the day so she didn't have her grandmother totally depending on her and eventually she knew if that happened she would resent her for it. She looked at him and shook her head, "Yes, you're absolutely right and if you can recommend some company that does that then I will hire them before she comes home. Could I get you to tell her that too? I don't want her to think that I insisted on that because I didn't want to be with her all the time."

He picked up her hand and held it in his as they walked into her grandmother's room. The doctor gave them time for their hugs and kisses then he sat down beside her bed. He took her hand in his, "Laura, I have some good news for you. I am going to let you go home in a few days as long as you keep up your exercise. Plan a schedule of walking and the time you will spend doing it. Make it a daily routine so that Faelynn will know where you are at all times when you are out for your walk. It will increase the strength in your legs. My one condition for your going home is for you to be independent. Therefore, I am ordering a full time nurse to stay with you until I am satisfied that you're going to be able to stay on your own. I want Faelynn to be able to continue her own lifestyle and not have to worry about you so much. Are you okay with that Laura? There is one other thing too and I want you to get one of those necklaces that if anything happens to you while walking you can summon help. Those are very specific rules you must follow and if you can do those then I will sign your release papers on Wednesday."

She looked at him and fully agreed to all his demands. She said eagerly, "Dr. Wellington, I will do my level best to wait upon myself and be independent. I would welcome the nurse to help me bath because it is difficult for me to do alone." She reached up and gave him a big hug. "Are you going to sneak off and come have lunch with me sometimes?" He gave her a big grin, "Of course."

Faelynn stepped closer to the bed and held her hand as the doctor examined her again. He made a big production of saying, "I now proclaim you, almost well, Laura Myers." They all laughed at him. He bent down to give her a peck on the cheek, "I want you to take care of yourself from now on because you're a special lady to me." She nodded and patted him on the cheek. He stood up and smiled at Faelynn and walked out the door.

She stared after him as did her grandmother, "He is such a fine young man, any grandmother would be so proud of him. I bet his mother and father are very happy with his chosen career." Faelynn turned to look at her grandmother; she had never made any statement like that as long as she had known her. However, she did agree with her.

Faelynn went to the other side of her bed and sat down. She wanted to bring up her parents so bad but at the same time she didn't want to hurt her grandmother by talking about them. She was more than surprised when her grandmother brought them up. She had stared at Dr. Wellington's back as he moved down the aisle and her grandmother said, "Your father was a lot like him. He was ambitious and hard working and so caring. He was always looking for something to make life better. He would have made a find doctor instead of an investor of sorts."

Oh wow, thought Faelynn, *This is my open door that I have waited for*. "Grandmother, what type of work did my father do? What kind of investments did he have? You know I really don't know much about my father or my mother. Can you tell me about them sometime?" She dropped the subject and went on to tell her about what happened in Oregon and with her boss and friends. It took the better part of an hour before her grandmother yawned again and needed to take a nap. She stood and watched her grandmother slide down into the bed. "I'll be back tomorrow morning that way it will give me time to get a few things done at home." She kissed her grandmother's cheek and walked out to the elevator. Dr. Wellington walked up to her and handed her a piece of paper with a phone number on it. "Call this number so you can set the help up your going to need." She thanked him as the elevator arrived and she stepped inside. He called out to her, "See you tomorrow same place," She laughed and replied, "I'm going to buy that bench and have it engraved." They both chuckled for a long time before he went onto another patient. There was another person that overheard their conversation and that was a very pretty nurse standing at the nurse's station. She sighed, *why, couldn't it be her? Then she went back to her duties.*

CHAPTER 8

Faelynn arrived home and let herself inside. She went to the office and moved the chair and pulled the plastic container out. She walked it up to her bedroom so she could look through it again. It was a most valuable find. She came downstairs to fix a light supper when the doorbell rang. She walked to the door to find a man in uniform there. She recognized it to be the delivery company with the things from her apartment.

She walked out to the shed and asked him to unload it there and she could bring it into the house one at a time and look through them. He was done in no time and she returned to the house. She fixed herself a large salad with a roll and a cup of coffee. There was so much to do in the house and so little time to do it now that her grandmother could be coming home in a day or two.

She walked up to her bedroom and looked through the room. There was so much work that should to be done and she was not sure she could live there and work on it. Then the idea hit her. Why not live in her parent's home while the redecorating was being done here. She could hire a firm to do it while she and her grandmother relaxed at the other place.

She flipped through the phone book looking for a decorator that could start to work quickly. She found two in the book and called them to see if they could work on such short notice. One couldn't but the other agreed to come to her house for a meeting. She brought swatches and samples for feeling and to choose from. She took her upstairs to see her room and they looked at the samples against the wall and floor. After her choices were made she asked for some references so that she might be able to have her start later that day. She had two written down and one was no other than Richard's mother.

She asked the girl if she could have a business card and would call her in a little while. The woman left, her name was Annett Bennett. She quickly called Richard and asked him about the woman. He started laughing so hard he almost teared up. "Didn't you recognize her? She went to school with us. Her name is Annette Helms she married my brother Jackie. She won't use her married name because she wants to earn the money for herself and not for the Helm's name." Faelynn thought for a minute and did remember Annette but she hurriedly asked him, "Is she good at her job?" Richard sobered and remarked, "She is extremely good at her job but pricey." She thanked him and quickly hung up the phone.

That was all the recommendation she needed so she called Annette. "Hello, Annette, Could you please stop back by the house as soon as you have some time?" Annett agreed so Faelynn went down stairs and put on some water for tea. She got down some light cookies to put on the tray. Now that Faelynn knew who she was she felt a lot better about working with her. She heard the doorbell and went to open the door. Annett walked into the living room, sat down on the love seat and opened her briefcase. Faelynn hear her teapot whistle, "Annette would you like a cup of tea before we begin?" Annette replied, "I sure would and thank you for asking." Faelynn left the room and came back a few minutes later with her tray. She served Annette and sat the cookie plate on the coffee table.

Annette picked up her paper, "Faelynn, this is a standard contract that I need to have filled out before we begin work. Then we can include the specific things you want to have done in the house." She handed the contract to Faelynn and she picked up a pen and signed and dated it, handing it back to Annette. Annett was surprised but went on to discuss the plans for remodeling the house.

They walked from room to room and Annette took notes as to what she wanted changed and what could stay the same. She explained to Annette, "I am going to move to my parents home while you redecorate but time is of the essence so be sure to hire all the people you can to get it done quickly. Even if they work twenty-four hours a day it doesn't matter, I can pay for it. I know it is short notice and I need it done quickly but I will pay for that convenience. I want to surprise my grandmother when she comes home from the hospital. Do you think you can get all that done in such a short time?

I don't want to do the major overhaul now just some facial treatment so it looks pretty for grandmother. It will lift her spirits a great deal. She is to be released from the hospital in a few days." Annette looked at the tall order, "I can do this and I have plenty of help so we should be done in no more than three or four days max. When are you moving and how can I reach you?" I will be moving tonight and the home of my parents is located a block or two over at 2942 Sycamore Street." Annette jotted the address down on her notebook. "There isn't a phone there so you'll have to have someone stop by with messages if you need me; I'm going to call the phone company to have a phone there when they can get to it." Annette said, "That is not a problem but I need to use your phone to get some people over here working." Faelynn started up the stairs, "I'll go pack and get out of your way. Here's the key."

Faelynn moved her plastic container and enough clothes to last her for a few days and moved into her parent's home. This would also give her the opportunity to go through some of the things inside there. It had all worked out pretty well all the way around. She opened the door and walked inside carrying the plastic container. She went back for her clothes and personal care stuff. She locked the door back and cut on the lights. Surprise they were on. She walked over to the phone and picked it up. My goodness it was on too.

She called Annette and gave her the number there. She looked at the refrigerator and it was on but empty. She would have to get a few things to eat at the market for at least three days. She thought it strange that her grandmother had never shut off the lights or phone. Why would she keep them on? Did she ever come here? There were even more questions to ponder. She walked into the bedroom and looked at the bed. The bed her parents had slept in. She walked to her room. It still had the little bed she remembered. The third room had blue curtains and a bed with a blue spread with rockets on it. The closet had new boy clothes hanging in it. She walked back out to the kitchen and looked into the cupboards. There were a few things in closed jars such as tea and coffee. She wondered how fifteen-year-old tea tasted like. She got a cup from the cupboard and heated some water for a cup. She stood in front of the china closet while she waited for the water to heat. She looked at each piece of the beautiful blue plates and cups with saucers. There were small figurines that her mother had collected and a picture propped up against a glass. She opened the door and took the picture out. She looked at it carefully and didn't recognize it as her. But who could it be? Perhaps it was her half brother? She took the small picture with her into the dining room. She sat down at the table and propped the picture in front of the saltshaker.

She picked the picture up and turned it over and there was a name, Mark, now she knew it was her half brother. She stared at his face, where are you Mark? What did you become? Did you have a good life? I can't wait to find you so we can explore our parents together.

She finished her tea and walked back to the room she would be sleeping in. She looked in the closet and found some clean sheets to make the bed. She looked at her mother and father's clothes still hanging in the closet. She touched her mother's dresses and ran her hands over her father's suits. How she missed them. She took her father's suit coat out and held it to her. Oh daddy, I wish you and mommy were here now. Why did you have to die so young? I was so lost when you died. There was no one to love me since then until now. I lost so much when I lost you. She lovingly put his jacket back into the closet. She knew that nothing was going to bring them back.

She had brought boxes from the express company so she could sort some of their things. She went to the dresser and opened one of the bottom drawers. She found her mother's things and looked through them one by one. She placed them in the box and went from drawer to drawer doing the same thing. In one of the drawers she found a small box with a baby ring in it. It had her name on it. She took it out and looked it over. It was sterling with her name engraved on the top. It was on a small chain and there was a piece of her hair tied in a neat pink bow. She laid it gently on the top of the dresser. She went to the other end of the dresser and opened the bottom drawer of her father's side. She went through it and placed the socks and briefs in the box. The next drawer was his tee-shirt drawer and she refolded each one and put them in the box. The last drawer was for his personal stuff. It had an old watch that looked like it might have belonged to his father Earl. There were several neck chains, tie tacks and cuff links. She found a money clip with a note in it. She stopped and read the note. It said; *be sure check back with lawyer upon our return from New York to be sure he set up the trust fund for Mark.*

Well, this is an enlightening note. Daddy has set up a trust fund for him like he did me. Of course, he had no way of knowing it because her parent's hadn't picked him up. They had died instead. So that means an attorney somewhere knows about the trust fund. She needed to find the paperwork where the trust fund was set up. Once she found that she might be able to find Mark. She went through the house with a mythological system sorting the important with the not so important things. When she finished the dresser she went to the chest and did the same thing. She found some things from her mother's family and an old family bible where her mother's mother had put their family tree in it. She kept that out so that she could look at it to see if she remembered seeing or talking to any of them.

She found nothing else in the chest other than more clothes so she moved to another room. There was a little office den room that had a desk and filing cabinet along with two bookcases against the wall. It also had two chairs and a small television that looked to be black and white.

She walked over to the desk and opened the drawers starting with the top left. There were several supplies such as clips, rubber bands, pencils and pens neatly stacked beside each other with small pieces of paper cut from larger papers for notes. Her father must have been thrifty to keep pieces of paper for his notes. She went to the next drawer and it was envelopes and stamps and letters. She picked up the letters and opened the first one. It was from the adoption service about Mark. *Yes*, she had a starting point. She took the letters and put them on the table next to her purse.

She opened the next drawer and saw several legal papers. She lifted them out and laid them on the desk. She picked each piece of paper up and read it. She could not believe her luck. There were the papers she was looking for. She read the second and third piece of paper. It was all about Mark, his trust fund, adoption and whom he had dealt with and their contact information. She walked to the kitchen with the entire file and laid it next to her purse.

She looked at her watch and went to the phone in the living room to call the lawyer. She spoke with his secretary who said he was with a client. She left a message for him to call her at the new number that she had some information that might help him find Mark. She went back to her father's desk and she opened the other drawers and found investment papers like the one she had given the attorney and the house papers. She looked at them to see when they bought the property. It seemed so long ago. She guessed legally the house belonged to her and Mark since his adoption had gone through. She hoped he had had a good life and that there was some happiness and love in his life. There hadn't been much in hers.

The phone rang and she picked it up, "Hello." It was the attorney, Mr. Robinson. She thought of how surprised he was going to be when she gave him the information. "I have found some other papers that make finding my brother, Mark, a little more easily. She read him the information from the letters and promised to stop by so his secretary could make copies of them." He replied, "I will get a hold of the detective right away and give him this new information. We might be able to find him pretty quick now." She thanked him and he thanked her and they hung up the phones.

She had added much more paperwork to his important file and was still adding when the doorbell rang. She looked confused, who could know she was here but Annette? She opened the door and found Richard and Alexandria standing there all cleaned up. She looked at him with a puzzled face as he said, "Oh, you don't remember, do you?" He continued, "The day you had the intruder we rescheduled our dinner date. Can you get away for a quick bite with us? Alexandria stood there watching Faelynn; she smiled back at her, "Of course I didn't forget our dinner date. Where are we going Alexandria?" The little girl looked up at her and smiled, "Smokey's barbeque, yum." All three of them laughed. She walked back into the kitchen and picked up her purse and the key and locked the door after turning on the porch light.

Richard buckled his little girl in while Faelynn settled herself in the front seat. He drove over to the famous new restaurant named Smokey's BBQ and Grill. They went inside and found a table by the window. The waitress came to take their order and brought their drinks. Richard couldn't seem to get enough of looking at her. He couldn't believe that she had let him back into her life. "How are you doing since you got back home? Is everything settled in Oregon now?" She smiled at him knowing he was wondering if she was going to leave again, "Yes, it is and I'm glad it is done and over with. My things have already arrived here and stored. Annette is working her fingers to the bone trying to get the house remodeled before grandmother comes home. I want to surprise her with a bright frilly room that looks brand spanking new to cheer her up." Richard enjoyed her excitement; "I know Annette is working hard because Jackie has taken a few days off to help her out with the heavy stuff." But he laughed about it.

Faelynn looked at Richard and he sure didn't seem to remind her of the young Richard she knew of so long ago, especially not the one that brought her home from the prom. He was quiet, relaxed, and easy going. He turned from looking at Alexandria to looking at her. She spoke before he did, "Richard, I have known you for many years but I have never really known you. Can we talk about you tonight? I would like to hear about your life and how you came to this point and nodded at Alexandria."

He looked at her for quite a bit before he began. "After you left I just hung out with some old friends and attended college. I hoped you would come back and we could settle our differences but you never came back. I admit I was so wrong on how I handled that night and I sure do apologize with all my heart for causing it to go wrong. Anyway, I dated a few girls in college but since none of them were you, we never lasted long. I went to the state college to get my degrees because I knew someday I would have to take over the family business and I would need a lot of knowledge to make it pay enough to support us all. I worked hard and saved every penny I could to buy the hardware business too. Jackie came into the business the minute he got out of college too.

Then when they couldn't get anyone to run for Mayor, I volunteered. It isn't the pay but it's nice to be able to help build our town up and attract outside businesses to open stores here, which brings more jobs to the people living here. I've lived here all my life and have never taken a vacation to look at the rest of the country except for when I was in the service.

Do you remember Doug Flake that I used to hang around with him and Jerry Winters? Well, Doug got sick a few years back and he asked me if I would do him a big favor. I told him sure without even asking what it was. He then told me about his girlfriend Jean, whom he had lived with for about three years. He told me that he had to watch her all the time because she was a drug addict and she was pregnant with his child. He didn't want the child to be in drug withdrawal when it was born so he had to stay right with her to keep her off drugs. I had told him I would do anything for him because he was my friend. He wanted me to take over watching over his girlfriend and when the baby was born to take it and raise it for him. He knew she wouldn't keep it if she had it and he wanted his daughter to have a chance to grow up to be somebody besides a drug addict. I swore to him I would do it and he passed away peacefully in a week after our talk. I took his girlfriend and married her and put her in a hospital where she couldn't harm the baby. She was under watch for twenty-four hours a day seven days a week. It cost a fortune but I did it. The girl carries my name but when she is old enough I will tell her about Doug.

After Jean had the baby, I obtained a divorce from her and we went separate ways. She had met another man with a motorcycle and they both had shot up and gotten on the cycle to ride out of town on a country road. They passed a cop doing eighty miles an hour and kept going faster and faster and left the road doing a hundred and fifty miles an hour and it burst into flames when it came down.

I have fulfilled my promise to my friend and I don't regret one day of it. It was the best thing that ever happened to me. I have never known an unconditional love as hers. If I'd had known how much fun fatherhood was I'd started sooner". He smiled at Faelynn as he finished. "That is about all there is to it." Faelynn gave a low whistle, "That is some heavy duty stuff. Remind me to keep you as my friend." She saw something cross his face and then it disappeared. He smiled back at her.

Their food arrived a few minutes late but it didn't matter. The waitress apologized as she looked across the crowed room. Alexandria took bites of her sandwich and relished the French fries. Richard gave an adoring look at Alexandria, "It is your turn, tell me all about your life." She laughed and smiled at Alexandria, "When I lived here, I had my nose stuck in a book and after I graduated I applied for several jobs across the country and landed one in Oregon. That was about the distance I wanted to be from Georgia, so I jumped at it. My grandmother didn't seem to care if I took it or not because there wasn't much love lost between us. So, I moved to Portland and started working for an advertising agency.

I did pretty well and had my own clients who wouldn't sign with anyone but me. The money was good but the beach was better. I loved the ocean and spent a lot of time there when I was off work. I had a few friends but not a lot. I was still pretty much the loner. I had one male friend named Michael. We occasionally dated and I thought he might be about to propose when grandmother got sick. Perhaps, it was my imagination because when I got back, he seemed to have found someone else. I'm glad for him because I wouldn't have married him anyway. And other than that, you can see I'm here again to stay. So guess it was meant to be that I am here." He reached over and put his hand over hers and said in a husky voice, "Faelynn, I'm so darn glad your back home, I could kiss you. Nothing has made me happier than to see you again.

I hope you will allow us time to get to know each other again. I think we owe it to ourselves to explore our friendship to see where it will take us." She laughed and explained how difficult that might be, "You might not like the girl I have turned into, stubborn, opinionated and independent, determined to do it my way." He said lightly then grinned, "I don't see a problem with that, as long as you ask me first." She laughed out loud, "Oh yeah, like that not is going to happen." Then they laughed again and Alexandria joined them in laughter.

The meal was finished and he took her back to her parent's home. He came in for a little while and Alexandria explored the little girl's room. Faelynn told her, "This was my room when I was a very little girl like you." Her eyes got big as she listened to Faelynn. She walked around in the room and rubbed her hands over the dolls and watched the stars overhead and sat in the rocker. She was very quiet when she was in the little girl's room. She walked into the little boy's room and looked around as well.

Faelynn turned to Richard and walked toward the kitchen, "Would you like to have some coffee or tea?" He followed her to the kitchen while she made the coffee. They sat down at the table and Faelynn turned to him with her surprising news, "Richard, there is something else I would like to tell you but I didn't want to say anything in front of Alexandria. I have just learned this week that I was not my parent's biological child. I was adopted. It came as quite a shock to me to learn that by accident but there is another piece to it. I have an adopted brother. My parent had adopted him but wasn't going to pick him up until they had returned from their second honeymoon in Europe. Of course, you know, they died in that plane crash and never got to pick him up. I have an attorney looking for him. I want him to know that my parents truly loved him and that is why they adopted him but was prevented from raising him by a premature death.

I just hope he had a good life and was raised in a happy environment, not like the one I had. My grandmother and I are trying to patch up our relationship now and I would like for him to share in it with us. I know that father opened a trust for him because he did one for me. I haven't used anything out of it except for my education. I worked to support myself since I was sixteen and never asked grandmother for a penny.

Richard stood and looked toward the hall, "I need to check on Alexandria, she's much too quiet." They walked into Faelynn's old room and saw the little girl lying on the bed fast asleep with a teddy bear in her arms. They tiptoed out of the room and went back to the kitchen. Faelynn seemed surprised that she fell asleep, "She must feel comfortable here." Richard agreed as he watched her move around the kitchen, "You have had quite a lot to deal with since coming home. I'm not sure I could have handled all that and the burglar too. Did you find out what ever happened to the nut case?" She thought for a minute then sighed, "No, but I do need to check with the police on him. I don't want him following me around and show up here." Richard realized he never thought why she had moved into this house, "How did you learn about this house. Did you remember it as a child?" She shook her head *no;* "I found this the same way I found the adoption papers. Some were stored in containers in grandmother's storage shed and some papers were stored here. Grandmother never took anything out of here except the food from the refrigerator. Everything else was left intact. She even left the utilities and phone on for fifteen years. Can you imagine? I guess I will never understand her reasoning. I guess that she couldn't bring herself to admit that her only son wasn't coming back."

It was getting late and Richard stood after Faelynn had yawned a few times, "I'd better get sleeping beauty home into her own bed. Can we drop by tomorrow?" Faelynn smiled and looked at Richard, "I have a few errands to do in the morning and to see grandmother in the afternoon. How about coming over here for dinner? I'll try cooking again; if all else fails we'll order out or is it in." Richard touched her cheek, "Then we'll be here around six thirty. You're sure you don't mind Alexandria coming along do you?" Faelynn hit him gently on the arm, "Of course not, we have something in common Alex and I." Richard thought for a minute, "You know I like, Alex better than having to pronounce her long name. I'll see if she will like it. Thanks and see you tomorrow." He went into Faelynn's room and picked up his daughter and hugged her to his chest. She was such a beautiful child. He was a lucky man. He gave Faelynn a peck on the cheek as she opened the door for them to leave. She waved by to him as he backed out of the driveway.

She went back to her father's office and checked the drawers again to make sure she had taken everything out. She moved his desk calendar on the top of his desk and found several pictures under it. She looked at them without recognizing any of them. Perhaps these were other children he was thinking about adopting. She turned the pictures over and saw names on them. She didn't know any of the names but would take them to the attorney first think tomorrow to have him check them out. She looked at them over and over and wondered how many other children out there had her parents adopted.

CHAPTER 9

Faelynn woke to the sun drifting through the window. She stretched like a lazy cat. She had slept like a baby with no worries or problems to solve. She dragged on her robe and went into the kitchen to get her coffee. She fixed her cereal and toast and sat down at the table. She looked through the adoption papers and found hers. She looked at it for a long time. She flipped the page over and read the mother's bio. She had attended school in a small town called Whitefield down near the west Georgia line where Florida, Georgia and Alabama came to meet. The report said that her mother had not finished school and was not married to her father Edward Slocomb. Faelynn's breath caught, this had to be a mistake? They usually didn't put father's names on the adoption papers. *Her real father is Edward Slocomb?* What are the odds of finding him in Alabama? So it seems that her brother and she were adopted from Alabama. Well, now she knows it wasn't from the same family. How did her father find the adoptive parents?

She picked up her brother's adoption papers and read the mother's bio. It said she was the oldest child of six. She lived in a small country area of Etowah and that she never finished school and went to work as a waitress to help her family provide food for all the younger kids. The father worked in a cotton mill and the mother took in sewing. Neither of her parents had much education. The father is listed as Lee Wilson from the same town. This is a find that should help the attorney find their parents rather quickly.

She got up to go get her shower and got dressed. She was making her to do list so that she could get some things accomplished. The first was she wanted to stop by the house to see how the remodeling is going. Then she wanted to go to the attorney's and check on his progress. Then to Sims to buy a few groceries for the house here and later today stop and see her grandmother. For a person who didn't work anymore she sure was busy. She walked back to the bedroom and stepped into the shower. There was so much to think about, her mind whirled with activity. She knew or felt she was getting close, so close and soon she would know who her brother was, where he came from and about his family. She wanted to observe him for a while before telling him about their parents. She was going to talk to Kurt, to see if he thought her grandmother might be able to hear some of the news she is finding out or should she keep her out of it for a while.

She dried her hair and dressed in her chocolate pants and beige shirt with a single necklace that belonged to her mother. She wore her hair long today so it would dry quicker. It came down to the middle of her back. Most of the time she wore it up to keep it out of her face while she was working.

She drove over to her house and saw Annette's car was in the yard along with three other cars. She got out of the car and walked inside. She could tell they had been working hard because a lot of the downstairs had already been transformed to look like an elegant turn of the century home. She was duly impressed. She spotted Annette in the midst of several workers with her swatches and designs. She saw Faelynn and handed them to another worker. Annette came over to Faelynn, "How does it look so far? Faelynn was extremely happy to see it taking shape so quickly. "I think it is looking great. Have you done grandmother's room yet"?

Annette knew she was anxious for that to be done first, "Come on let's look." They walked up the stairs and Annette opened the room. Faelynn walked into her grandmother's room and just said, "Wow." Annette had taken grandmother's old bed and had it refinished to a rich warm brown almost the same color it was when she lived there. It was put closer to the window so that she could see down to the street. The window coverings had been all taken down and replaced with beautiful hand crocheted drapes. The side table also had a matching pattern of the crocheted tablecloth. The old rocking chair had a new cushion covered with the matching pattern, as did the throw pillows that lay in front of the big pillows on grandmother's bed.

The room was open and airy, with very little furniture moved from it. Lace and crocheted doilies adorned the furniture around the room and the beautiful old paintings of her parents and grandparents adorned the walls. It would be like stepping into a turn of the century house where she could have started out her housekeeping days in. She turned to Annette, "It's beautiful, I'm sure she will love it. I'm going, so I can get out of your hair now. Call me if you need anything." Annett waved to her as she pulled out of the driveway.

With her brief case beside her she headed to the attorney's office. She walked into the office of the attorney and signed in for her meeting with him. She looked around at all the clients he had sitting there and thought, he must be a good attorney or all these people would be somewhere else. Or, he had them sit there to impress his other clients. She smiled and thought no, she was right the first time.

The Secretary stepped into the room and called her name. She looked around but got up and followed her into the inner office. She showed her into Mr. Robinson's office. She put the briefcase in the next chair. After a few minutes he came into the room and sat behind his desk. She started to speak but he beat her to it. "I have some good news for you and that is, we have found your brother. We know where he lives and what he does for a living and he is a very well liked man. Would you like we can arrange a meeting with the two of you so that you can get to know each other?"

She sat up in her chair; "No, I would like to observe him for a little while before I talk to him. Does he live near here? From what I have found in my father's drawer we both were adopted from Alabama, different towns of course. There must have been some kind of orphanage there for my father to adopt us from the same place." She opened her briefcase and took the papers out and handed them to him. He handed her a folded piece of paper, which she stuck in her briefcase. He buzzed his secretary and when she came in he handed her the paperwork, "Please make copies of these she that she may take the originals back home with her.

Faelynn placed her hand over her briefcase and looked at him, "Were you able to find any other investment accounts? She pulled a paper out of her case and handed it to him. I also found this in my father's drawer. It seems to have several more accounts than you had listed." He looked over the additional accounts and mumbled to himself. He should have found these. He buzzed his secretary again. He handed it to her for another copy. His secretary came back with her originals all folded and handed them to her and she handed the duplicates to her boss.

He looked at this stranger that had become a millionaire in front of his eyes, "Would you like some coffee or something to drink?" She shook her head *no* and waited for him to go over some of the paperwork. Faelynn had decided to wait to ask him to find their parents until another time. She wanted him to stay focused on his main job and that was finding her father's accounts. He read the list of investments and checked them with the one he came up with. There were four other accounts and they were with very popular stock firms. He lifted his head and looked at her, "Okay, I will get on this to find out where they are and how much they are worth. I should get back to you in a few days or a week at the most. She stood as if to leave but said, "I found one other thing and handed him another piece of paper, this is the bank where it was opened. It is a trust for my brother. I would like to know how much is there and what kind of trust it is.

She thanked him for his time and walked out the door into the lobby. There were still a lot of people there, if they were all waiting to see Mr. Robinson they were in for a long wait. She got into her car and drove through town to the local grocery store. She purchased quite a lot of food for one person but she knew that Richard would drop over sometime in the near future. She enjoyed being with Richard because the conversation flowed smooth and easy like old friends. Sometimes it seemed that she had gotten upset over nothing but at the time it didn't seem like that to her. She guessed they would just be friends for now. She did love Alex to come over and visit with her too. She sure did like the short version of her name.

She drove into her driveway and took her bags of groceries into the house. She came back to get her last bag and her briefcase. She locked the car and went into the house locking it behind her. She became conscious of the fact that she had just locked her door in Covington. Never before had it been necessary. She cut on the porch light and went to the kitchen to put the groceries away. She laid her briefcase on the table so she could come back and take the papers out and put them into a safe place. She walked down the hall to her bedroom to take her shoes off. She was tired, it had been a long day but she was seeing some improvement at the house under Annette's supervision and the attorney is working hard for her. Oh, she jumped up from the bed and ran into the kitchen. She had remembered the folded note the attorney had given her, the name of her brother. Her hands trembled as she slid the case over to her. She pulled out a chair and sat down. The overhead light was on and she reached for the folded note and closed her briefcase. She was a nervous wreck and so anxious to see whom her brother was and where he was. She gently opened the folds of the note and looked at the name that was printed there along with an address.

She stared at the name on the paper and she began to cry, her whole body shook with the flooding grief for the lost family. Her parents had lost both of them; her and her brother and they had lost good loving parents who would have cared for them for all their lives. She didn't remember how long she sat there crying but she did hear a knocking at her door. She brushed the tears away and stuck the note in her pocket. She walked to the door and saw none other than Dr. Wellington. She opened the door and he stepped inside. He looked at her face and knew she had been crying.

He took her hand and asked gently, "Is there something I can do to help?" She shook her head *no* and let him enter the room. She grabbed a Kleenex and wiped her tears away. He walked closer to her and lifted her chin. He took the Kleenex and dried her eyes, "Now tell me what is wrong and how can I fix it?"

They walked inside and sat at the table. She reached over and closed her briefcase and pushed it to the far end of the table. He looked around the house, "Now, why are you living here? I thought you lived on Walnut." She looked at him for a minute before she started talking, "I'm having grandmother's house remodeled while she is in the hospital and hopefully it will cheer her up when she comes home. I'm having a lot of her antiques restored and put back into her room so she can enjoy them again." He looked at the inside of the house, the kitchen shelf with the old ceramic dolls, "Was this your home?" She looked at him as he looked the living room over, "Yes, this is my home, when I was a small girl. My parents owned it. Would you like to see it?" He stood up and she walked him through the rooms explaining who had lived in that room or what it was for. She stopped at her room and showed him her toys, her furniture and clothes, still hanging in the closet, as they were the same day she left there.

They walked into the boy's room and he looked around that room. She looked at him as he looked at the room, "This was my brother's room." He looked at the room several times shaking his head, When I was a kid I would have killed to have a room like this." They walked into the parent's room and she showed him the picture that they had taken prior to their death. She explained how they had died and how much she had missed them. She told him of how she lived at her grandmother's house and how lonely and unloved she felt. She explained how she had run from the problem and ended up in Oregon working there.

They walked back into the kitchen where she made some coffee for the both of them. She asked him an unusual question,

"Can we talk about your life growing up and whom you lived with and how you came by your last name." He gave her a curious look but agreed to tell her. He started by saying that he didn't know his last name or his father's. He was put in an orphanage when he was young and lived with a bunch of other kids that also had no parents. He was told that his mother had left him at the orphanage and he had been given the last name of Wellington because that was the administrator at the time. A lot of kids had the names of the workers, there because they didn't know the last names of the people that brought them into the orphanage. He explained that the longer he stayed there the more determined he was to leave. He studied hard while at the orphanage and learned as much as possible from the books they had.

When he turned eighteen they released him onto the street, "Good luck, you're free to go now." The first thing he did was to go to a hospital and asked for work. He was given a janitor's job and he got to stay in one of the empty rooms there. He saved his money and studied all the books he could get his hands on and before long he was able to get into night school. Once the doctors found out he was trying to better himself they would save their old books for him to use so he wouldn't have to buy books.

They would bring him their old clothes that still had a lot of wear in them so he would have some decent clothes to wear to school. Pretty soon he was graduating with honors from the school and then he enrolled in a college near the hospital. He kept working and studying and living on practically nothing when he got his medical degree and had gotten his license to practice. "It took me about the same time as it did the other people but I went to night school every day it was open, because I couldn't go to day school due to the work schedule."

She began to cry again and he knelt at her chair and begged her to tell him what the matter was and why was she crying. She went to the other end of the table and opened her briefcase. She picked through the papers and separated them on the table. She handed him a set and she had a set. He looked at the adoption papers and looked back at her. He held the papers in his hand and was turning them slowly, "I guess I don't understand what these are for because I've never seen them before. They don't have my name on them." She quickly looked at him and replied; "Oh, but you didn't know your name, remember?" he smiled and said, "Yes, I remember." He looked to her for an explanation though.

Faelynn choked back her tears," Kurt, you are my brother. My parents adopted you and it was all finalized. They were going to pick you up when they returned from their second honeymoon in Europe. The problem occurred when their plane went down in the Atlantic Ocean and no survivors were ever found." He looked stunned, as if he had been punched in the gut. How could this happen. He had a family, yet he lived in an orphanage where no one loved or wanted him. He looked at her thinking she must be mistaken, "Are you sure? Why didn't someone claim me, if I was adopted?"

Faelynn only had answers for a few questions, but she took out the detective's report and handed it to him. It was about him so he should have it. It gave all the information that he already knew about where he lived and grew up and the orphanage name. The report had names that he should know or those people who gave birth to him and gave him away. Tears formed in his eyes, the tears of a hundred years flowed from him that night. All the anger, frustration, loneliness and hurt slipped out of him and fell to the floor. They held each other and cried for a long time, comforting each other. When they stopped he looked at his adoption papers again. He walked back to the boy's bedroom and stood inside it for a long while. So this room was to be mine. I would have loved it here. Why was I cheated out of my life here?" Faelynn didn't know but she did know that he had hurt as much as she had.

Faelynn asked him another personal question, "How long have you been a doctor?" He replied to her in a low voice, "Only for a year or so. I just got done with my residency and this is my first full year." She smiled because she knew something that was going to shock and surprise him, "So, you aren't wealthy and still have to scrimp by?" He admitted that was true. "All my money goes toward my bills, student loans and the only charity I can afford or will afford and that is to help children try to have some kind of joy in their lives." She smiled at him and said, what he hadn't said, "Because we didn't?" He nodded his head in agreement.

She went to her dresser and picked up one last piece of paper for him. She handed it to him and he read it slowly. She whispered, "Our father even opened a trust fund for us before we came to live with them. You have a trust fund. We just have to find it. I have hired an attorney to find you, once I knew you existed. Then, I found the trust fund information and the attorney is looking for it, for you. I already have mine and we both own this house together. Do you own a home of your own? He looked up at her and laughed, "You must be kidding. I barely own the shirt on my back. The only reason you and I went to the country club dance is that we were invited as special guest of someone who wanted me to join the club. They don't know my back ground or how poor I am."

Her curiosity was getting the best of her then. "Where are you living now then? Do you have an apartment?" He smiled and shook his head, "No, I still live in a room at the hospital."

She went to hug him again. Oh Kurt, you can have this house and I will move back to grandmother's house." Kurt looked at her for a moment, he couldn't believe what has happened to his life but right now it was turned upside down. "Faelynn, will you do me a big favor? Can we stay in the house together tonight? At least spend one night in our parent's house as brother and sister. I think it would make me feel more like your brother and like their son if we could." She followed him back into the living room where they sat and talked for more than an hour. They laughed and cried for the parents that loved them and for their loss. They were elated at being able to connect at last.

They sat up for most of the night talking and each one told their story so that it could help to bond then. Kurt told of when he came to realize that his mother and father didn't want him and how he came to the orphanage. "I know there had to be some reason but I never knew what it was. What I don't understand is if I was adopted once why they didn't try to adopt me out again. Why just drop me off at an orphanage and forget me. They must have gotten some money when our parents adopted me. Why didn't they use that to keep me?" He rubbed his hands over his face and let out a big sigh. "I just don't understand. I guess I never will."

Faelynn looked at him trying to think of a way to help him find the answers to his questions, "Do you want to have the attorney find your parents so that you might ask them some of the questions that still wonder around in your mind?" He looked at her for a minute, "Yes, I do want to know where they are and get the answers to my questions, but not right now. Faelynn, I'm in such shock that I'm still reeling from the shock. Here, I was trying to date you and come to find out you're my sister. This is really something to swallow all in one gulp. I mean, did it take you this long to get used to the idea that someone wanted you?" She stood and walked to the kitchen and put on some water for tea or coffee.

She said over her shoulder, "Kurt, I think it shocked me as much as it is shocking you now. I just found out about me just the other day so this is new to both of us. I always thought that I was their natural child. I never dreamed I was adopted too. But the more I think about it the less it bothers me because I know one thing for sure. My mother and father truly loved me even if they didn't give birth to me. I promise you this Kurt; they would have loved you unconditionally too. They wanted you or they wouldn't have gone to the trouble of adopting you. So, we are their children. I'm just grateful they found us and wanted us.

He shook his head in agreement because he finally knew someone really did want him and loved him. He now felt the loss that Faelynn had known. Then, he grieved the loss of the two most important people in the world, his parents.

He got up and walked into the kitchen and sat down while she got their drink. Faelynn thought of another thing for them to discuss. She turned to face him when asking, "Do you have to work tomorrow?" He was already trying to figure out what she was thinking, "No, it's my day off, which is why I came by to see you. I went to our grandmother's house and they sent me here. I wanted to ask you if you wanted to spend the day doing something together, but I guess not now, huh?" Then they both laughed. She handed him another cup of coffee and sat down with him. She opened the brief case and pulled out the other pictures and showed him. She wanted to share some of her father's thinking with him, "I found these pictures under father's desk calendar but I don't know who they are or if our parents had adopted them yet or not. This is something else we need to check on. We might have more brothers and sisters out there that need us to guide them through this new experience we're having.

Kurt jerked up his head and sat up straight in his chair, "Oh my, Faelynn, Oh my goodness." He was getting really excited as she watched him. "Do you know what this means? It means that I have a grandmother too. I have a grandmother. Oh my goodness, I can't believe my luck. I loved that little old lady in the hospital and now I find she's my grandmother. How much luckier can I get?" Faelynn just smiled, "It's just the top of the ice cream, and you'll know a lot more tomorrow."

Faelynn set her cup of tea down on the table, "That is a subject we need to talk about too. When my parents left me at her house to go on their honeymoon and didn't come back. It was the most miserable time for me, I felt as if grandmother didn't love me or care if I lived or died. She all but ignored me the whole time I had lived there. That is why I kept my nose in a book hoping to get my college education so I could get as far away from her as possible. By the time I finished college I had my trust fund and had paid for most of my education. I looked for jobs on the other side of the states so she wouldn't have to see me, nor I her. She kept in touch but only with polite letters. I didn't know she was really sick until you contacted me. She never told me. When I came back I realized how important she was to me. She was my only living relative. At the same time I didn't know I was adopted either. So I made up my mind that we were going to bond together one way or the other. After seeing her every day and living in the house. I found some of daddy's papers in the shed.

As I went through them I realized how much she had been so hurt when her only child had died. It must have cut her heart right out of her chest. She had been devastated and unresponsive. To a child living in her home; that had also lost her world, was not a good combination. She couldn't give me the love I wanted and I could replace her darling son whom she had loved with all her heart. So she turned inward and neglected the child.

Her husband, grandfather Earl had died a few years before and he was the rock of the family. He loved grandmother so much that he gave her anything she wanted. She had told me that he had even raised father so she could keep up her social activity in the community.

I can see now, that I have been back for a while that she truly does love me but I think she feels guilty about not being able to give me the love when I needed it. As I said, I want this relationship to grow especially now, now that we have found you. I want us all to bond as a family no matter how it came to be. I know grandmother loves you she has said so. She even said she wished daddy had been a doctor instead of an investor. So she is pleased with your profession. Now, we have to figure out a way to bring it all out to her without upsetting her. So think, brother and let us see what we can come up with."

Faelynn got up from the table and walked back to where she had stored the photo albums she had found here and brought them to the table. She handed Kurt one and she took one. He opened them and looked at all the pictures of the family that her father had taken of them when she was a baby and as she grew up. She turned to him; "Just picture you in these photos because that is the way it would have been if they had lived." He looked over at her and smiled. It was still hard for her to believe, she had a brother.

Faelynn looked up from the album, "Kurt, there is another person we need to talk about and that is Richard. I'd like to tell you the story of why we split up so long ago. He had asked me to go to the prom with him. I was so much in love with him I couldn't see strait. All he had to do was smile at me and I'd swoon. We went to the prom and it was so beautiful and I felt so special because he had asked me. It was probably the happiest day because there hadn't been any prior to my daddy and mommy.

On the way back from the prom Richard pulled off the main road on a side road and wanted to make out. I guess he didn't realize my background and I told him in no uncertain terms that I was not that kind of person and wanted to go home. I think now that I was just terrified of someone touching me like that since no one had even hugged me in so many years. I fought him off and he took me home. He tried to call me the next day to apologize but I told him never to call me again. We have dated a few times since I came back and we talked about that night and he got his chance to apologize for upsetting me. He told me he had no intention of dishonoring me, that he has always been in love with me and no one else has interested him since I left. He also told me that he had planned on proposing to me that night." Kurt popped up and asked, "But wait a minute do you know he has a child?" She smiled at her brother, "Yes, I have met her and know the story behind her. She is the child of a very dear friend of his that died. His wife was pregnant and was on drugs.

He asked, Richard to take care of his wife and his child. Richard took his promise seriously. He married the wife and had her locked in a rehab center until the baby was born. At least putting her there kept her off drugs so the child wouldn't be having withdrawal from her mother's addiction. Anyway after the child was born the mother took off with another man and they were high on drugs and they were traveling at a high rate of speed when the motorcycle left the highway. They both were dead.

He adores the little girl you can tell immediately. He has made a very good father for her and she is safe and will have a happy normal life. Someday I hope to share that life with him but right now I have to get my own life straightened out." He reached over and covered her hand with his, "Faelynn, if you love him let him know. He'll help you get through whatever it is you're having a problem with. He is a very nice guy and I like him a lot. Although, I did enjoy dancing you around at the country club with his jealous sparks flying everywhere." He then laughed long and hard as his eyes sparkled at her.

Faelynn looked out the patio door and saw the sun coming up. She turned to her brother for input, "Do you want to get some sleep before we start our day or wait and sleep tonight?" He stood and walked to the door and looked out. "I think there is too much going around in my head to sleep. I'll catch enough tonight, I'm used to sleeping only a few hours a night."

Little did either of them know that a car sat outside with a man sitting at the wheel watching the house and its occupants? His hands were gripping the steering wheel but his heart was breaking. He slowly eased the car into the street and drove home. He knew he couldn't take heartbreak like he took before. He loved her too much to try to keep her. He would leave, yes, that was the answer. He would go away and try to get over her again. He would let her go so she could be happy.

CHAPTER 10

Morning came and Faelynn suggested they get their showers so they could go do some errands she had planned. Kurt knew he had no clothes there, "Why don't you get your shower here and I'll go back to my room and get mine and change and you can pick me up there." She thought for a minute then replied, "Great idea, then we could spend the day together." He reached and pulled her into his arms. I don't think I've been happier to lose a girlfriend, but gain a sister. There's just no comparison of the depth of love I feel for you. I knew when I first met you there was something special between us. I felt the same with our grandmother. Isn't it funny how we feel a connection without knowing about it?" She put her hand on his arm as she related, "Now, that lovely nurse on the fourth floor can chase you for a while." He looked at her mystified, "What nurse?" Faelynn slapped his arm and growled at him, "You know the one, Miss Brown eyes." He realized which nurse she was talking about. "She does flirt with me now and then. Maybe now, I can flirt back." Then he roared with laughter. Faelynn agreed to pick him up in an hour so that they can get some of their affairs settled. He left her standing at the door after one more hug. He laughed and asked, "Will you pinch me to be sure I'm not dreaming?" She pinched him real hard as she scrunched up her face. He yelled, "Ouch!" She laughed out loud, "See you're not dreaming." He walked to his car with a lighter step and a happier heart. He had family; something he had wanted for so long was now his.

She got into her shower and dressed as quickly as possible so they could start to unravel some of the mystery of his family. They would get breakfast first and then see the lawyer and then to the bank. They might even visit a car lot or two to see if he could use a better car than that old piece of junk that he had. Doctors needed a new flashy car to drive if for only their reputation. But she knew he was too sensible to splurge on something foolish. He had lived lean for too long to be wasteful especially, with his father's hard earned money.

She drove into the hospital parking lot and saw him sitting on their favorite bench. She walked over to him and he stood up. She threw her arms around him for all the doctors and nurses to witness. She didn't care, he was her brother and she was so proud of him.

They walked hand in hand out to her car. He laughed at her as they reached the car, "Are you trying to give me a bad reputation?" She laughed right back, "No, I don't have to do that because YOU already have a bad reputation." He laughed and opened her door, "Uh oh." They got into her car and drove out of the parking lot. Those dark brown eyes watched as the loving couple left the lot. She signed and walked into the hospital to her fourth floor desk.

She found the little café in town and pulled into the drive. They walked in the café hand and hand. The waitress sat them in the back corner. They could see everyone coming into the café while they talked. They placed their order and waited as their coffee was being served. Faelynn looked at the cup of coffee then at Kurt. "Oh no, not another cup of coffee," and they both broke into a fit of giggles. Their food came and they talked quietly as they ate." Kurt, I know your car isn't the best, or that dependable. Don't' you think you should have a better more dependable car?" He looked at her then smiled, "Why is that big sister, you going to buy me one?" She smiled at him, "Me, Absolutely not!" He threw his hands up into the air and replied, "Then I don't need a new car do I? You're the first person I have dated in over a year, I live in the hospital, I have no gas expense getting to and from work so therefore, I don't need another car." She just knew he'd be like that, stubborn and hard headed two traits she would learn to love about him.

After breakfast they made their way over to the attorney's and as she signed in for them, he found them seats. He looked around and couldn't believe the people that were sitting in his office this early in the morning. Faelynn walked back to sit next to him and she too looked around the room. She leaned close and whispered to him, "The attorney pays these people to sit here so it makes his office look busy. See who they call next and then you'll believe me." Mr. Robinson's secretary came to the door and called Faelynn into the office. She whispered to him, "See, I was right."

They both took a seat in front of the attorney. He looked at Faelynn and smiled, "I see you wasted no time in contacting your brother." She smiled back at him, "No, I didn't, since we had dated a couple of times I figured it was time to tell him who he was." The attorney's eyebrows raised a half-inch at her statement. She smiled, "Shock" yes, that worked.

We're most anxious to see if you found his trust fund. Then we have a few other things to go over with you." She reached into her purse, "Oh and here is the check for the first few things that have been completed." The attorney took the check and looked at the amount and buzzed his secretary. She came into the room, he held the check up and she took it from him and walked out the door. He smiled at her backside as she went. He whispered, "Damn, good secretary. Almost reads my mind." Then, he pulled out his file and went over it with her. He pulled some papers out of his file, "We found the trust fund and it is at our local bank here so you can contact Mr. Davis and he can go over it with you. I have taken the liberty of calling him to advise him you would be in to see him. Do you want to know what's there or should you wait until you see him?" Again, she got the folded piece of paper from the attorney. They stood and walked out of his office. She tucked the piece of paper into her jacket pocket to look at later. Faelynn wanted to surprise him.

When they got to her car she asked Kurt to take over the driving, "Can you drive, we need to get some gas too. I'm a little nervous." Kurt got behind the wheel and they went to the first gas station to fill her tank. He got out and pumped the gas for her. She slipped the note out and looked at it. Her hand shook. It was over three million dollars. Her father was an investing genius. No wonder Kurt is getting the country club invitations. She laughed to herself. *He is really going to be surprised; boy is he going to be surprised.* To think he has scrimped and saved all his life and he was already rich. Goodness, she thought, what if they had never knew about him, had never found him. To think he could have gone to the best schools and had a fairly good life, if he had only knew about the money. She hoped it didn't change him too much or for him to go wild and spend it all in a short time. She would encourage him to leave most of it in the investments.

He got back in the car and they drove to the bank and parked. It didn't open for a few more minutes so they sat there talking. "Kurt, if you suddenly won the lottery what would you do?" He rubbed his chin and thought, "The first thing I would do was to get me a newer car." He grinned at her then continued, "Then, I'd get a home of my own and put a lot in savings and investments and lastly I'd do what I could to help other kids, whose parents didn't want them, to find some happiness in life. I think it's important for them to laugh some and not have to be worried about surviving through each day. Faelynn looked over at him, "You have a good heart, my brother. I'm going to be so proud of you."

She handed him the paper the attorney had given her. He stared at the paper for a long time before unfolding it. He looked at the amount written there and looked at her. He wiped his eyes and then his face, "Are you serious, this is what my trust fund is? What did our father do or invest in to make it grow to this amount?" She looked at him struggling to hold in his excitement, "Our father was a very savvy man when it came to making money. He knew what to invest in before those smart men on Wall Street knew what was going on." He bent his head over his hands on the steering wheel. "Just think I could have had it so much easier, had I had this money to live on." Then he raised his head and looked at her for a moment, "No, I probably would have wasted it all. By going through the hardships, I've learned to appreciate money more." He reached over and took her hand, "Thank you, my sister for not giving up on finding me, for caring for me and wanting me in your life. I love you." She held his hand too, "I love you, my brother, now we are a family and our grandmother is going to be so pleased."

They walked into the bank and went straight to Mr. Davis's desk. He motioned for them to sit down. He hung up the phone quickly, "I've been expecting you. Mr. Wellington, Mr. Robinson faxed me copies of the paperwork proving that you are Miss Myers's brother, so I can get the funds disbursed to you in a few minutes. First, I'd like to find out how you want them divided". Kurt looked at him and at Faelynn. Faelynn look at Mr. Davis and gave him instructions, "He'd like one million in checking and the rest to stay in the investment account." Mr. Davis looked at Kurt, "Is that what you want Mr. Wellington?" Kurt shook his head *yes* and smiled at Faelynn as the assistant mgr left his desk. He frowned leaning close to her he whispered, "Is that really what I want, Faelynn?" She knew that he needed some spending money to get some of the normal living expenses taken care of and his school loans cleared. "Yes, Kurt you need some money available to you if you want to buy something on the spur of the moment instead of having to come back and ask for it to be transferred again. You have some outstanding student loans to clear up too. So yes, you will need some extra funds for things like that. The other money will grow back very soon so enjoy having money in your pocket for a while."

They shared a smile while waiting for the checkbook on his account. Faelynn did think of another thing she would talk to him about when they were alone. Mr. Davis came back to his desk and handed Kurt his checkbook and his passport card. He told him all he had to do if the bank wasn't open he could use the teller with that card. He wrote down the code he had keyed in and handed it to him. Kurt stood and shook his hand. Mr. Davis said to them both. "If there is anything I can do for either of you day or night, here is my card don't hesitate to call me." They thanked him and left the bank.

As they got into her car, she asked him, "Kurt, since you really don't have any special attachment to your last name why not have it changed to your legal name. The one that father gave you? I know you'd probably like to keep Kurt but how about Myers for your last name?" Kurt thought about it for a while, "Dang, little sister I'd love that. Can we get your lawyer friend to do it for us?" She laughed thinking of the money she was giving him, "He's no friend, he charges money, but yes, he can do it. I think daddy and mom would be so proud to see that you were finally theirs."

Faelynn asked, "Would you like to go out to grandmother's house to see how the remodeling is going and then we can have lunch somewhere. He got behind the wheel and drove them out to their grandmother's house. They walked into the house and stopped and looked around. It was beautiful. It was like walking into a grand mansion at the turn of the century. Faelynn couldn't help but feel honored to be standing in the entry. She was sure that Kurt felt the same way because he was just standing there staring. She touched his arm bringing him back to the present, "How do you like the remodeling job? All he could say was, "wow, it's magnificent." A few minutes later she saw Annette coming out of the kitchen. She looked like she was having a problem. Faelynn looked at her thunderstorm face, "Is everything all right Annette?" Annette looked at Kurt unsmiling, "Can we speak alone in the living room?" Faelynn said certainly, she turned to Kurt, "Can you go out to the shed and pick up another one of the plastic containers and put it in the back seat of the car?" He looked at her and knew they wanted to speak alone so he left the room. She followed Annette into the living room as they both sit down on the sofa. Annette was twisting something in her hands. She knew she was nervous, "Annette, what is the matter. Has something been delayed in shipping? Is there problem with your help?" Annette looked at her straight in the face, "No, it's a problem with my brother-in-law Richard." Faelynn looked alarmed, "Is he okay, he isn't hurt or anything is he?" Annette was surprised at her alarm after Jackie had told what Richard had said to him. Annette continued, "Richard is gone, he left this morning and said he didn't know when he would be returning. He said he might send for Alexandria to join him later on but he wasn't sure he would be coming back here." Faelynn put her hand over her mouth, "Did he say why? Where would he have gone?"

Annette looked her right in the face as she replied, "I know why he left but I'm not sure you want to know why he left." Faelynn looked at her strangely, "Why wouldn't I want to know where he went. We have been seeing each other again for the past few weeks." Annette looked at her thinking the worse, "Yes, but you've been seeing Casanova during that time too, especially last night." It suddenly dawned on Faelynn and she realized Richard has assumed something that had not been what it seemed. She needed to set Annette straight so there would be no rumor running about town about it. Annette, "I found out quite by accident when I moved back here from Oregon that I had been adopted at birth. My father couldn't' have children so he adopted me first then he adopted Kurt. Only neither Kurt nor I knew it. Since moving into my parent's home did I find both of our adoption papers, I have had an attorney looking for him. When I found out it was Kurt, I was shocked and so was he. He was raised in an orphanage in Alabama.

The adoption papers had been completed but my parents weren't to pick him up until after their return trip to Europe. As you know they both died in the plane when it crashed into the Atlantic Ocean and there were no survivors. When I found the adoption papers for the boy I didn't know who it was but we came from the same area in Alabama. The detective found Kurt and when he came to see me last night, we sat up all night going over everything that belonged to our parents and talked about all the things we had missed in life even though I was living with them when they died.

My grandmother was so upset after her husband died and then her only son that she couldn't cope anymore than I could, so we co existed in this house until I was grown and moved away. So you can see that Kurt is not my lover but my brother. Richard misunderstood the situation and should have knocked on my door and it would have all been explained to him. I just wish that Richard had more faith and trust in me before he left. The only reason I'm telling you Annette is that I know you won't be spreading it around town to be gossiped about. Annette patted her arm, "Faelynn I'm so sorry that I misinterpreted the situation as Richard did, perhaps he will come to his senses before he makes a complete fool of himself. I'm so sorry, I know you've had your share of problems since your parents died, it wasn't easy for you." Kurt walked into the living room and saw how distressed Faelynn was and walked over and put his arm around her, "Is everything alright sis? Do you need anything?" He looked at Annette and wondered what she had said to upset his sister. Faelynn walked outside with him and they got into the car. She told him of the conversation with Annette and what Richard had done. He looked at her with sad eyes, "I'm sorry Faelynn. I knew he was jealous of me but I didn't think he would go this far. To walk out on the person who loves you is downright stupid." He tried to make her smile. Should we go find him and drag his sorry butt back to your door and make him apologize for hurting you again?" A sad smile came on her face as she shook her head, "No, it was his decision to leave and it will have to be his decision to come back to hear an explanation from me." She tried to cheer them both up by suggesting something near and dear to their heart.

"Well, what should we do now? Let's go car shopping."
They drove down the auto alley like two kids that had just been
handed the kids to daddy's car. They looked and looked and
salesmen followed them around like pups waiting for a bone.
But neither of them could find anything they really needed.
Faelynn laid her arm across her face as she exclaimed, "Oh
no, the miser has came out in Kurt and he is not going to be
able to part with his money." They laughed and giggled so bad
that they had to leave to get some lunch. After lunch they went
to the hospital to see their grandmother. As they walked into
the room she spotted them. He released her hand and walked
over to his grandmother. "How are you doing today? Are you
feeling well?"

She replied, "Yes, I'm fine, I just got back from my trek
around the hospital. With a good looking man on my arm too."
Kurt put his hand to his mouth and whispered, "Shocking,
older woman steals hospital aid's heart in strange love
triangle." They all laughed so hard that the nurse came into
the room to see what the problem was. Kurt looked up to see
whom it was and was staring at Miss Brown eyes. He smiled
at Faelynn. Then he turned to the lovely lady with brown eyes
and asked, "Say, how about you and me walking down to the
cafeteria and have a drink together and set some tongues a
wagging around here. The gossip is getting old and is usually
wrong, of course. He smiled and wagged his eyebrows at her
and she too burst into laughter, "Dr. Wellington, I never knew
you had this mad comic side. I accept. I'll be right back before
you change your mind."

Faelynn and Kurt chuckled as she walked out the door. He
did a good imitation of flipping a cigar through his finger like
a comedian, "Guess I'd better get to the elevator before she
leaves without me." He bowed to the ladies in the room and

went out to prop himself against the elevator door. Faelynn's grandmother looked at her and then at him. She was surprised to see them laugh and joke together, "What in the world was that all about?" Faelynn looked at the couple by the elevator before turning back to her grandmother, "It seems Dr. Wellington has had a secret admirer for some time and has just found his funny side. You'll see a lot more of him, like that I'm sure."

She sat down beside her grandmother," Do you remember the other day when we were talking about my father? Can you tell me more about him?" Her grandmother looked pensive and began to talk. "When your father was just a young man he got the chickenpox and he had a very hard time with them. When he finally got over them the doctor said he probably wouldn't be able to have children. He was really crushed over that because with him being an only child he wanted to have many children.

For some reason the pox at an older age makes the man sterile. He devoted his time to studying because he felt he would never marry that no one would want a man who couldn't produce children. He was so wrong. He had known Caroline for most of his life but he avoided her when he found he couldn't have children because he knew she wanted them. When he fell in love with your mother it was like a Cinderella story. The more he saw her the more he fell like a ton of bricks. He fought the attraction hard but in the end he gave into it. The first thing he did was to tell her there would be no children. She came back with the retort that there could be a thousand children if they adopted. Well, the more he thought about that the more he loved her. Knowing she would love him on any level with or without children. He couldn't believe the gift he had been given. They married soon after that and had been devotedly happy ever after. That is why they were going to Europe for the second honeymoon. They were going to look at another child to bring into their family.

Faelynn said in a quiet soft voice, "Why didn't they or you ever tell me I was adopted?" Her grandmother reached for her hand to hold, "I couldn't, you see before they left they made me promise not to tell you no matter what. They had intended to adopt several other children and would tell them all at once when the children felt secure in their home. They adored children and wanted them to be loved in return. Your father was a very good man at investing and he had amassed quite a sum of money. He opened you a trust fund even before you came to live with them." Faelynn was afraid she was going to cry before she could get out of the room. "Grandmother, I think that I need to leave now so that I can do some thinking.

Do you mind if I go through the storage shed out back. I saw some of father's papers when I stored my things from the apartment in Oregon there. I would like to read them to be close to him again. I know he loved me because they showed me everyday how much they cared for me. I know the entire group of brothers and sisters they would have adopted would have been made as welcome as I was." Her grandmother looked at her with loving eyes as she said, "Faelynn, whatever is in that house is yours to do whatever you want to with it. I would have told you if not for the promise. It didn't matter to me how many children your parents would have adopted they still would have been my grandchildren. If I'd had any sense after Jack's death I would have told you anyway. But I wanted to die with them; I wanted to be with my husband and my son again. I wasn't sure I could go on living without them being there for me. They were my heart and I worshipped the ground they walked on. I hope we can repair the damage that I did to our relationship, if you can forgive me I will try my best to make it up to you."

She bent down and kissed her grandmother on the cheek, "We're going to be fine grandmother, with determination on both or parts we'll make it just fine. I'm just trying to sort out some of father's affairs." She squeezed her hand and walked out the door. She waved to Kurt and his favorite nurse as she walked out into the sunshine. She knew what she was going to do. She was going to move back to her grandmother's and let Kurt have their parents place. She would be living there when her grandmother came home anyway so why not let Kurt have his own place to live. It will sure beat that hospital room he has been living in for the past umpteen years.

She swung into the driveway and pulled the boxes she had picked up inside with her. She went to the back room again and cleaned out her clothes from the closet and her personal care things from the bathroom. She took the sheets off the bed to be washed and dragged them into the living room and stuffed them into a box. She walked to her old room and looked at the clothes in the closet. She had brought a box for each room. She emptied the closet and carefully placed the clothes in the box. She went through the drawers and did the same thing. She went to the dresser and looked at the tiny little pictures that were sitting on the top. This was her life; she would cherish these things her mother had left her. She looked around the room and folded the box top for someone to pick it up. She walked into the boy's room. She started to do the same but decided to let Kurt do it so she left the box in the middle of the room. Perhaps they could donate them to the orphanage that Kurt had come from. She would try to find out where it was even if she had to make a trip out there. That might be a good thing for both her and Kurt to do.

She called the hospital to see if she could find her brother. They located him in his room. She told him about what she thought they should do with the clothes in their rooms and he wholeheartedly agreed. Her mind was whirling with ideas they had discussed. "See, if you can get some more days off and we'll drive over there." He called her back and informed her, "Pick me up." He waited for her outside the hospital. She drove in and he walked to the car and got inside. They drove across Atlanta on I-285 then dropped off onto I-20 headed west to Alabama. They found the town soon enough and did some asking around and found the small little house where Kurt had began his life. She wasn't sure she had lived there too but probably did.

They walked to the door and knocked several times. A thin wrinkled woman answered the door. They could hear the babies in the other rooms. It sounded like several women were with them. She looked around the woman to see the inside of the house, "Is there anything I can do to help you? Are you looking for a baby? We have plenty right now". Kurt asked her, "Do you run this place, "No, Reverend Johnson does and he is the one you would have to see about getting a baby." Kurt asked another question, "Where do you come by all these babies. Does the state put them here?" She was getting weary of his questioning, "Oh no, folks around here are so poor they can't afford to have any more children so if they can't keep it they bring it here. Sometimes, young girls decide they can't take care of the children and adopt them out through us." Kurt tried to be casual but wasn't, "Does the government know your adopting these children out?" The old lady looked at him real funny and decided he asked too many questions so she sent him to the Reverend, "You'd best talk to Reverend Johnson for anymore questions cause I rightly don't know the answers but he will. Kurt asked another question, "How can I contact Reverend Johnson or where was his office.

She pointed to a bigger house that sat at the other end of the block. They got back into their car and drove down to the other house. They were sure that he had been forewarned. They knocked on the door; an older woman who invited them inside opened it immediately. They stopped inside the room and it was very much different than the one at the other end of the street. It was immaculately cleaned and the antiques were of the best quality. She took them to a sitting room where they waited for the Reverend. After a lengthy few minutes, he appeared in the doorway all cleaned up and ready to do business. The Reverend introduced himself and went to his desk and sat down. Faelynn talked first. She looked at the man behind the chair and tried to figure out just how much it would take to buy his records. "Reverend Johnson, we are from Covington Georgia and have just recently found out that we were probably adopted from this very place. We would like to know if there are any records that you have that go back to about fifteen years. The Reverend thought for a minute about what these two wanted here. They were dressed well so his housekeeper had thought perhaps they wanted to adopt but looks like they only wanted information. He wondered how much they would pay to know who their real parents were. He cleared his voice as started to speak, "Well, yes, we do have records back that for but they are all stacked in buildings and would be hard to locate. Why don't you give me the information and I can look it up and send it to you, for a fee of course. Faelynn stood and walked to his desk and placed her hands open on the desk as she leaned into him.

Reverend Johnson, I am a very wealthy woman and I would be willing to make a substantial donation to this organization to see my brother and my record. Are you interested in a trade, Reverend?" The Reverend wiped his forehead. He liked this woman; she got right to the point, money. "Well, yes, of course we take donations and if you give me your information I'd be glad to go look for it right now." Faelynn turned around toward her brother and smiled as she picked up her purse with their adoption information in it. She gave the Reverend a copy of each one, "We will be waiting right here when you return. That will be soon won't it Reverend? I'll just sit here and write out my donation check while you're gone." He muttered a few words and hurried out the door. They heard the back door slam and heard another one open in the back of them.

Kurt walked over to her and pulled her off the sofa and they walked to the front door before speaking. He whispered, "You're wicked." She just smiled. He whispered again, "I think the room is bugged because there is a wire down the leg of the sofa. Perhaps, they leave clients alone to discuss the children and listen to them somewhere in the back." They walked back into the room and saw the housekeeper coming out from the back of the room. She had to come from somewhere inside because they had watched the door and no one had gone inside. They sat on the sofa humming until the Reverend returned with their paperwork.

The Reverend returned in record time with the files. He resumed his place on the other side of the desk. He opened the folders and read them. He looked at Kurt with a funny expression, and then he looked at Faelynn. He looked at them both, "I thought you said this was your brother?" Faelynn calmly replied to his query, "He is my brother because my father adopted us both." The Reverend looked at the next page and then said, "Oh, okay now I see. Yes, your father was interested in several of our children and we had hoped he would have taken a few more of them. I had sent him several pictures of other children that were available at the time. He supported the orphanage for several years before but his checks just stopped coming."

Faelynn informed him of their parent's death, "It was because he died in a plane wreck in the middle of the Atlantic Ocean. But he left his children well heed when it came to money and investments." The Reverend was writing on a tablet and ripped it off to give to her then, "You did mention a sizable donation, right?" Faelynn looked at the Reverend, "That donation included the entire file for me and my brother. No file no money. I can hire a detective to get the information I want if I have to." The Reverend knew she was right. What did it matter? The files were old and no one else would be interested in them anyway. He then agreed and held out his hand for the check. Faelynn stated mater of factly "I am going to be sending the orphanage some clothes and beds for the children. I will make surprise visits to the orphanage and it had better be cleaned and the children fat and healthy from the food you're going to get them. My auditors will be here once a year and audit your books. Should you not allow the auditors access to your books. I'll have the government on you so fast they will close you down in a heartbeat. Are we clear Reverend?"

He began to sweat again. He knew she was going to be trouble, "Yes, Miss Myers, we're clear." She turned around just before leaving to advise him of her gift to the orphanage, "Your first shipment will arrive in a day or two. Make sure that pigpen is cleaned over there and hire some more women to watch those kids. When the clothes arrive they'd better be bathed too. They will have a bath at least every other night. The inspection team will report to me if the standards should drop. We're going to support your orphanage, Reverend, but it will be kept up to our standards." She stopped and walked back over to him and pulled the check out of her pocket and handed it to him. He looked at the check and fell back down in his chair with his mouth open. She turned and walked out of his office with two files in her hand. When they were back in the car Kurt turned to her, not a minute longer could he wait to ask. "So what did you give him?"

She was reading the files already but looked at him, "Oh that, it was for one hundred thousand USA dollars." Kurt jerked his head around to her and yelled, "What! You paid that much money for those two crummy files?" She looked at him very calmly. "Don't you think having your parents address was worth that? Or knowing who my parents were and where they lived was worth that? We would have had to pay the detective agency that and they would have spent it in luxury hotels." Kurt calmed down somewhat, "Yes, you're absolutely right. Especially, since it was your money." Then he chuckled. She laughed then too, "Oh, didn't I tell you we're splitting the cost?" He looked at her and smirked, "Then next time you get the urge to buy files let me do the talking. I'd have beaten it out of him." She went tisk, tisk; we don't stoop to violence now, brother of mine." They both had a good laugh.

She pulled an Alabama road map from the dash of her car. She looked on the map to see which town came first. She saw Etowah about twenty-five miles ahead of them as the crow flies. She took her pen and drew a circle around it. She looked at Kurt and pointed to the map, "Looks like you get to see your parents first. Etowah is straight ahead of us about another twenty-five miles or so." He shook his head but didn't say anything. The miles ticked off as they listened to the music drifting in over the radio. They started asking each other general and personal questions. She started by asking, "What is your favorite singer?" He would answer, "Hank Snow." She would look at him and he would ask, "What is your favorite thing to do?" She would answer," Reading," It went on and on like that until they reached the small crossroads of Etowah. They slowed down to look it over and finally pulled off the road. They spotted a little café and pulled into the parking lot. He looked at her thinking, how many cups of coffee they could stand and made a face, "Can you stand another cup of mud?" She looked at him and bristled, "Coffee yuck!" Then she smiled at him, "Yes, because we're one step closer to seeing them."

They entered the café with roadmap and folders in their hand, looking like typical lost tourist. They each ordered coffee and sat in a booth pretending to be looking at the map. When the waitress brought their coffee, they asked about a family named Hollister that lived in this area. She stopped and thought, "I don't remember a Hollister but let me ask the cook he's been here since God was invented." She smiled and walked back to the kitchen. In a few minutes a big burley man came to the table. He didn't look too friendly either. He had arms the size of Kurt's legs and spoke like a sailor, "You looking for the Hollister bunch? Faelynn gave him a big smile, "Why, Yes sugar, my friend said she lived down this way and I was on my way to my grandmother's in Whitefield and thought I'd stop by here first." She had coated that last sentence with such a southern drawl that Kurt looked at her too. Of course, that got a grin from the big burley guy, "Well, honey, they live right down highway 21 until you get to the white church and you turn left there and it is about three miles on the left. The big old green double-decker farmhouse can't miss it pretty lady. She gave him a big smile as they stood up to leave. Kurt took out the money to pay for the coffee and the big burly guy was still smiling at Faelynn. "Ah heck, ain't no charge for coffee, it's on me." Kurt thanked him and took Faelynn's hand. He was still smiling at Faelynn when Kurt pulled her out of the café and back to the car.

He didn't say one word until they were well away from that café then he busted out laughing. "Girl, I thought that guy was going to kidnap you and take you home with him." She laughed too before saying, "Well, it got us the address didn't it?" He kept laughing as he shook his head. "Yes, but I could visualize myself lying in a gutter somewhere beaten to death trying to save you." They laughed for quite a while about that until Faelynn saw the white church at the crossroads. They made the left turn and started looking for the farmhouse. It came into view and Kurt slowed the car. They drove by it slow and looked it over. It was a broken down farm that looked like only a few nails held it together. There were several kids playing in the yard and two women out digging in the garden. There were no more than one or two poor looking cows and a slump back mule for plowing the fields. It was a sad way to make a living. He could imagine the half starving kids that lived there and his mother had been one of them. A man came out from inside the house and walked toward the women. He glanced up at the car and Kurt was able to see that it was him that he favored.

The older man was tall with overalls a big floppy hat that covered black hair. It looked like he wore those overalls over his long johns. They drove slowly on by the farm as Faelynn looked over at him. "You're not going to stop Kurt?" He looked at her and replied, "No, I just wanted to see it. I'm not ready to deal with it." She understood that. So they went back to Hwy 21 and turned left again and headed down to Whitefield. They rode in silence for a while before seeing the sign for Whitefield. They rode slow through town and were surprised to find it a very nice and homey place. They went to the motel and got two rooms side by side then went in search of a place to eat dinner. The clerk at the motel suggested, Gene's steak house two blocks down the street, so that is where they headed.

When they arrived they discovered it was a steak house on one side and a bar and grill on the other. It had a connecting walk through hall where the restrooms were installed. They found a table and the waitress came right over to take their order. She brought their drinks and left to wait on other tables. It looked like the place locals would come to a lot. She asked the waitress when she came with their meal if she knew any Slocomb's that lived around there. The waitress replied quickly and without hesitation, "Oh Yeah, Ed Slocomb works down to the auto shop and his wife Kathy works at the beauty shop. Then she asks, "Are you related to them, kin from out of town?" Faelynn had to think quickly as the waitress probably knew them personally, "I used to know someone that lived in this area and had introduced me to a Slocomb but I couldn't remember their first name. But thanks so much I appreciate it." She quickly turned to talk to Kurt to stop further questions. Kurt smiled at her because he knew she was having the same problem facing them as he did, "Brave going little girl. You almost found out something." She looked at him and frowned, "We are just not cut out for this type of thing. Perhaps we should leave the investigative work to the professionals."

Kurt looked around the room as he chewed on his steak, "Wouldn't you even like to have a look at him?" She nodded, "Yes, but I'm not sure I'm ready to talk to him. Perhaps at a later date I might get the courage to ask more questions. I would like to have some answers too but not like this." They looked at each other for a long time.

CHAPTER 11

Kurt looked at her and took a big drink of his tea, "I think we should take a drive by of the auto shop first thing in the morning and then head back home. Our grandmother can be brought home as soon as we get back." She turned to look at him, "Yeah, let's do that. This is enough exploring for me. I'm ready to go home too." He looked at her thinking, "Do you want to leave tonight?" She looked at him over her glass of tea, "You're not too tired of driving?" He laid his napkin down beside his plate and reached for his wallet. "Heck no, let's get the heck out of here and go home." He paid the bill and they walked out to the car and drove back to their motel and tossed the bags in the car trunk and left.

They got to their grandmother's house around three in the morning. She told him, "You can sleep in the guest room if you want too, this way you can you don't have to drive any further tonight." He thought it was a good idea too so he took his duffle bag inside with hers. She was at the stove heating hot tea for both of them.

They sat at the table sipping their drink when she apologized, "I'm sorry, I led you on that wild goose chase. It was really a dumb thing to do." He looked at her and smiled, "No it wasn't a wild goose chase because we now have our records and know for sure where they are and what they do. Sometimes that is enough for a while." She sat in deep thought, "Yeah. I looked at the towns we're from and they are dirty, and life was hard there, I think we were lucky to be adopted out of that place. It would have been a no win situation for us or our parents." Kurt agreed.

They cut off the lights and walked up the stairs. He went to his room and within a few minutes she could hear him snoring. He was exhausted from that long drive but wouldn't have admitted it. She turned over in her bed and went over the things that they had done and thought what a waste of time that trip had been. Well, other than at the orphanage. She was sure that when she went back there she would see a much cleaner place. She wondered how they ever made it out alive from that place. She thanked her parents for finding her and adopting her and Kurt.

She lay there for a long time just thinking of things and how they had changed her life and how she felt about it and what she was going to do about Richard. She knew he was hurt but so was she. Instead of coming to her and asking her for the truth, he chose to leave their relationship and go off alone. He didn't even trust her to tell him the truth. What kind of relationship would that of been, to have him suspecting her if any male came near her, even if it was her fault or not, she'd be to blame. Would he be wondering if she had had an affair with them? That kind of jealously could quickly kill a marriage. She'd rather live by herself than live in a marriage like that.

She didn't want a love or marriage like that and if that was the way Richard was going to be then she would be better off without him. After thinking for a little while more she finally drifted off to sleep to the lullaby of her brother snoring in the next room. She awoke to the ringing of the phone. She picked it up and said, "Hello." The voice on the other end sounded like Richard, but she couldn't hear him very well.

She said, "Hello, I can barely hear you can you speak up?" the line went dead. That was an odd phone call. She got up out of bed and put her housecoat on and went down stairs to fix some coffee. It was still early so she let Kurt sleep in. She was sitting at the table waiting for the coffee to get done when the phone rang again. She rushed to the phone, "Hello." There was no answer but the line was open. She repeated, "Hello, Please speak louder I can't hear you. Richard is this you. Are you all right? Where are you?" The line went dead again. She was getting very frustrated and worried. The voice, what she heard of it sounded like Richard but she really couldn't be sure. She would call the Helm's once it got daylight and ask about him. Let them know what happen and perhaps one of the men knew where he was and go check on him.

She heard Kurt getting up, so she poured them each a cup. He came down the stairs and met her at the table. He looked around the kitchen at the new appliances and modern cabinets, "From what I've saw of the house so far it looks great." She looked around admiring the new cabinets and appliances, "I hope grandmother likes it. I tried to re-create some of her past to put back into the house. Something delicate and fragile as a love from her past so she can see how it looked when she first came here." She motioned for him to go with her, "Bring your cup and come up and see her room." She knew he hadn't looked at it yet. She wanted to share the thrill of seeing their grandmother's new room. He followed as they talked about the changes she had done with each room.

She opened the door and the look on his face was priceless. He walked to the center of the room, "This is so beautiful, and it looks like I've walked back into the previous century." She watched as he admired each piece of the hand crocheted décor. "That was the effect I was going for. Do you think grandmother will like it?" They each walked around in the room touching the beautiful pieces of lace admiring how well the room turned out. He turned to look at her, "I think she will absolutely love it, I do." She blushed and replied, "I didn't do it for a man's room, just grandmothers. I wanted her to feel special when she saw it." He put his arm around her, "She will absolutely adore this room. It is a special room for a special lady and she will know it was done with love."

They walked back down stairs and as they reached the kitchen again the phone rang. Faelynn picked it up again and didn't say anything but just listened, it sounded like someone was hurt and calling for help. She was sure the voice was Richard's. After the phone went dead she called Jackie, Richard's brother. She told him of the four phone calls "The last phone call I got just a minute ago sounded like Richard. It sounded like he was hurt. If you or anyone knows where he is, can you go check on him to be sure he is alright?" Jackie hesitated but admitted, "We have had the same experience just a few minutes ago. I'll see if I can find him. We couldn't figure out the calls we just thought it was a prank caller. But you're right I'll see if I can locate him to see if he is all right. Thanks for calling Faelynn; I appreciate your concern for him."

She sat down at the table with a concerned look on her face. Kurt knew she was worried about Richard. He patted her hand, "Jackie is a good man; he will go look for his brother. Someone from his house surely knows where he went. He has a child he just wouldn't leave and tell no one where he was going. Richard is more responsible than that. If that child got sick, they'd know where to find him I'm sure. What do you say we go over to the other house and do some more exploring?"

She walked up the stairs and got into the shower. She dried her hair and dressed and went back down stairs to fix a light breakfast. They ate cereal and toast with strawberry jam and had coffee to wash it all down. Faelynn hoped that Jackie would find his brother unharmed. She felt saddened because of Richard's decision to leave instead of talking to her. She hoped and prayed he would be okay. She washed up the dishes and as she was drying her hands the phone rang again. They looked at each other as she picked up the phone. Jackie was on the line talking loud and fast. "We've found out where he is and are on our way there now. I'll call you once we get back." She gave him the other phone number and he said he'd call both when they returned. She thanked him and hung up the phone.

She finished wiping her hands and picked up her purse and went out the door with Kurt. They went to the other house and as they walked inside, there seemed to be a chill in the house. She asked Kurt, "Do you feel the chill in here?" He wrapped his arm around her, "It's just your nerves sis. Don't worry; Richard will be all right now. You alerted his family to his potential problem and they will find him. You've done all you can do."

They walked back to the girl's room and brought the box of clothes from it into the living room. She had brought the tape, marking pen and paper to list what was inside. Kurt went to the boy's room and found a box waiting to be shipped. She knew he would want to be alone there so she found something else to do in the kitchen.

He took each outfit from the closet and looked at it. He gently placed it in the box; this went on until all the clothes from the closet were gone. He moved to the dresser and opened the drawers from the bottom up. He felt each little tee shirt and diaper. Placing them in the box along with the brand new clothes he would have worn had he been brought home to live. The many pictures that were on top of the dresser were tiny miniatures of him. There was a little welcome note from his parents telling him how special he was and how much they loved him already. He put his hand over his eyes and wept for the love he never had and the regret of never living with his beloved parents. He picked the few pictures and walked them into the large bedroom where he would be sleeping and put them on the dresser there. Those were something he would keep forever and hand down to his children when they were old enough.

When he finished he picked up the box and took it to the living room so that Faelynn could mark it and label it for the orphanage in Alabama. They would go shopping for more things for the kids in Alabama to make sure all of them had enough clothes and clean beds and blankets of their own to keep them warm. He saw Faelynn standing in front of the china hutch and he walked over there to stand with her. They looked at it for a while before talking. He knew she was missing their parents, "Do you want to take these?" She looked at him with loving eyes, "No, I want you to have them. I had a piece of mother and father's lives; you didn't get to share that so I want you to have their dishes. They will bring harmony to the house. They belong here." He kissed her on the cheek, "Thank you for being such a good person. I fell in love with them the first time I saw them. They seem to fit in the house, like they are sitting there waiting for mother to put them to use for our dinner. I didn't get to share their lives but this house has so much love in it that I can feel them here."

Faelynn nodded saying what was in her heart, "I think they're happy that we're together and know that we knew they truly loved us as their own." Kurt moved to the table and looked on the shelf above the stove at the little trinkets. "She must have collected everything. I feel more like part of the family in this house. I think it is because they lived and loved here and some of it is still here." The phone rang and Faelynn picked it up but before she had a chance to talk Jackie was yelling through the phone. "Faelynn, we've found him. He's had an accident and in bad shape. The ambulance is taking him to the hospital now. He was on his way home and ran off an embankment. I have to tell you Faelynn it looks bad. Try to get to the hospital as quick as you can." And then the phone went dead.

She turned quickly to Kurt and relayed the message, "They found Richard, He's had an accident and on his way to the hospital now. Jackie says he looked bad and be prepared for the worse." Kurt grabbed her hand and she grabbed her purse and they were on their way to the hospital in seconds. They got there just as the ambulance arrived. She stood and watched them take him out of the ambulance and saw blood everywhere. Kurt had gone into the emergency room and was barking orders to the personnel. They had an operating room ready by the time he was wheeled inside. Kurt examined him and sent him to surgery. He went upstairs and scrubbed because he would be performing the surgery on Richard. The man his sister loved so he'd better not make any mistakes or miscalculations.

Faelynn sat in the waiting room for hours with the Helm's family without any word on how he was doing. She told Annette, "I'm going up to my grandmother's room and if you hear how he is doing can you send an aid to get me?" Annette agreed to do that and Faelynn walked up to see her grandmother. She walked into the room and sat by the window. Her grandmother was out walking again. Diane Nelson the head nurse for the fourth floor stopped by and they talked for a while. She tried to assure her it would be ok but Faelynn wasn't so sure. She wasn't sure of anything anymore.

After a few minutes she saw her grandmother coming back into the room. She greeted her with a hug and a kiss on the cheek. She tried to make conversation to stop her from thinking so much, "How are you doing? Are you about ready to start climbing up and down stairs?" Her grandmother held out her hand and Faelynn took it, "News around the hospital travels fast. I know Richard is in the operating room. I just hope and pray everything will be all right and he will come through this." She patted her grandmother's hand, "I hope he comes through it too, grandmother, because if he doesn't, I don't know what I will do. You see I've fallen in love with him all over again. There has never been anyone but him that was important in my life." She hugged her granddaughter and whispered, "That is how I loved my Earl. There wasn't one part of my heart and soul that he didn't fill." They stood there for some time just holding each other. Then the nurse came into the room to see if they needed anything. Faelynn shook her head because she was too choked up so she whispered, "No, not at the moment. We're going to just sit here and talk for a while but if you hear from Kurt or if the operation is over please let us know." The nurse nodded and left the room.

"Grandmother, do you mind if we talk about mother and father. I feel close to them now and would like to share some of my memories and discovered some finds that have answered a lot of questions for me." Her grandmother replied, "No, child you can talk about them and I'll be glad to listen. There is so much I blocked out when Jack died maybe it will help me to hear it."

Faelynn stated. "When my things arrived from Portland, I had the driver store them in the small shed at the back of the yard. When I opened it I saw boxes and plastic containers filled with papers. I took one in the house and went through it. It had belonged to father. It had a lot of financial papers in it and it had my adoption record. That is when I learned I had been adopted. It was so devastating to me that no one had told me about it. Then I found mother's diary. I haven't read it all yet but I am going to. I found another legal document and it was another adoption record. It was for a boy. It didn't really say much but just that my parents had adopted a little boy. I also found an address with the papers that was just a few streets over. The address was 2942 Sycamore Street." Grandmother sucked in her breath when she recognized her son's address.

She whispered, "That was Jack and Caroline's home when you lived with them." Faelynn nodded, "Yes, but that was so long ago and I was a very young girl. I had forgotten where we had lived. I found a key that didn't seem to go to anything on your key chain so I tried it at that address and it opened the door. I wondered through there and found my room and all the lovely memories of my parents came back to me. I cried for a long time for the love I lost when they died. I spent time there for several days and went through father's desk and found more papers. I found my full adoption records and I found my brother's adoption records. I went to an attorney and had him find my brother. He called me a few days ago and I went to his office and he gave me the name of my brother. I was shocked and surprised to find that I knew this man and he was a very nice man. "I hope you will love him as I do, because we're going to be a family, the three of us.

His name is Mark Anthony Hollister. But since father and mother could not pick him up he was transferred back to the orphanage home and given a new name. He lived in a dirty shack where there were too many kids for three women to look after and he had no one who loved him. We went to find our adoption papers and we were able to buy them from the orphanage for the right price, of course. We went looking for our parents, what we saw scared us half to death. Neither of us could make contact with them because we were afraid of rejection again. So, we drove all the way home from Alabama without stopping for anything. We have been together for the last three days talking about our parents and what we want to do with our lives now. He is a wonderful man and I couldn't have picked a better brother myself. We get along so great and I'm sure you're going to be so proud of him too. As a matter of fact that is why Richard is in the hospital. He came to our parent's home while my brother was there. He thought, he was my boyfriend and got jealous and left our relationship without even asking me about it. He assumed I was having an affair with another man and didn't trust me to be true to him. I started getting strange calls and knew the voice sounded like Richard and he was in trouble. I called Jackie and they found him, after he had gone over an embankment on his way back home.

I don't know if we can ever straighten this mess out but I do feel I have to be here for Richard, in case he needs me. It was me he called so he must have had a reason. I just hope he lives through this so he can raise his little girl.

Anyway, my brother and I have done a lot of talking and soul searching and we have definitely bonded. We stayed at our parent's house and went through the paperwork of father's and found pictures of other potential children they almost adopted. We are going to be monitoring the orphanage and if anything looks wrong I'm going to call the government on them and have them closed down. They work on the edge of illegal and they need to give those children a better place to live. We're going to see that they do. We've donated all the clothes from both our rooms including the furniture to them and had it shipped already.

"Grandmother, did you go into the house often?" Her grandmother sighed and nodded her head 'yes', "When it first happened I did. I would go there to cry. I missed Jack so much; he was all I had left of his father's and my love. I would have done anything to bring them back. It broke my heart to have to live when I knew I'd rather be dead. But I finally figured it out that I couldn't leave, it was because I had a mission in life and that was you. I know it took me a long time to realize what it was but none-the less I finally knew. That is why I offered you the house if you would return here, which you flatly refused. So, I sat and waited hoping you would come back of your own accord."

Faelynn reached over and patted her hand knowing she had suffered so much by their loss. Then she continued; "When I was going through the plastic container I found my parent's wills. Father had willed everything to mother and she had willed it to me. So that means that the house they lived in belongs to me. Do you have a problem with that grandmother?" Her grandmother shook her head, *no.* "That is good because I gave it to my brother alone with mother's dishes, which he loves already and all the funny knickknack's she collected everywhere we went. He walks around the house like I first did, touching everything that belonged to them. He was trying to keep a memory of them, hoping to feel the connection in all their things. It has been such a joy to find him and for the attorney to find his trust fund. It has been here at our bank all along. Father opened it when the adoption was final."

She saw a movement and looked at the door. Standing there was Kurt in his scrubs He had come to find her. She ran into the safety of his arms, "Is it over?" He held her close and patted her hair. He choked out her answer. "Yes, it is over and he lives to fight another day." She cried as he held her. Diane stepped inside the door and laid her hand on his arm and he nodded and smiled. She knew the results and sighed. She was relieved to know it went well. She turned to go but he stilled her with his hand. She looked into his eyes and stood beside him. Faelynn turned to her grandmother with tears streaming down her cheeks, "Grandmother, this is my brother and I love him so much, I hope you will share our happiness at finding each other." Diane and their grandmother were surprised at the news but it took their grandmother less than half a second to react to the news. She walked over and put her arms around both of them and said, "Welcome home, my grandchildren. I love you both so much and am blessed this day with a miracle." They all hugged and Kurt was so happy to finally find his family.

Kurt took Diane's hand in his, "Faelynn, Grandmother, I want you to welcome another addition to our family. I've asked Diane to marry me and she has agreed to live in our family home. I've told her all about my life and how we came to discover our adoption papers and I also told her how thrifty I am, so she will get used to it." He then smiled at Faelynn, and she rolled her eyes. Faelynn hugged her and kissed her on the cheek as her grandmother did and welcomed her to their ever-growing family. Diane looked up at Kurt with bright eyes, "I have loved this man since he first came here and couldn't seem to get his attention." She then looked at Faelynn and put her hand on her shoulder, "I'm happy that both of you have found such a cherished bond." Faelynn squeezed her hand and smiled knowing that she was going to be a close sister.

Faelynn turned to Kurt for information of Richard, "Is he in a room yet?" He squeezed her hand, "No, in ICU." I'll walk down there with you. He kissed Diane and his grandmother as they left the room and took the elevator to the second floor. When they arrived there they found Richard's family all sitting around waiting for him to wake up enough so that they might be able to see or talk to him. Faelynn took a seat near them and Kurt walked into Richard's room. He spoke with the nurse and attending doctor there and checked Richard's vital signs before returning to the waiting room.

He sat down next to Faelynn and spoke to the family. "I have just checked Richard and after some extensive surgery a little while ago he does seem to be improving somewhat. It is going to be a long road for him because he suffered a lot of damage from the accident. He broke his leg, his ribs cracked and one punctured his right lung. He has a mild concussion and he was very dehydrated. He was out in the elements for at least two days. He needs a lot of rest and I think it will probably be two or three days before you can talk to him. You can see him through the window but in his shape and the testing he is going to have to endure over the next two days will tell us a lot more. But he is alive and is on a slow road to recovery. I don't think more than one or two people should stay here at a time. I'm only thinking of Richard's stress if he should see a lot of people milling around the window. I know you're all anxious for updated conditions and I promise to keep you informed. I know you love him and want to be near him but please give him the space and time to heal. He will be in ICU for several weeks and visiting hours here are very limited so check with the nurse as to what time they are. Only immediate family can visit him. I have your phone number Jackie in case there is any change and you need to be contacted. Otherwise, if you all will get your information from Jackie it will save all of us a lot of time.

Faelynn bent her head because she knew that she could not visit him she was not immediate family. But she would get her information from Kurt. That would have to do for now. She was just grateful that he was alive. Kurt looked at her and whispered, "Don't worry, I'll keep you posted." He stood up to leave as a nurse came through the door and called to him. He walked back and they stood talking then Kurt walked back into the ICU to Richard's bed. He stood there for a few minutes and walked back out. He sat next to Faelynn again and talked in a low tone. Kurt looked at his very tired sister and whispered, "Richard wants to see you now. I've told him I don't think it is wise for him to see anyone yet, but he's insisting." Faelynn put her hand over his, "You know I would love to see him but I don't want to cause him more pain than he is already in." Kurt whispered, "If you don't see him now he won't get any rest and will make himself worse." She bent her head before saying, "All right for just a minute. I think Jackie should come in too because he called us both for help."

Kurt looked up to see several of the family watching him. He stood and said, "Jackie, Richard is asking to see Faelynn, it could be because he called her for help when he needed it. I am going to allow you and Faelynn to see him for a minute but nothing else until his two days of testing is done." They both followed him into the room. The nurses stood back for them to be on each side of the bed. Richard spoke to Jackie in a ragged whisper, "I can't thank you enough for finding me and getting me here. I love you and tell everyone I will be fine." Jackie held his brother's hand and replied, "Take care and rest and know we love you." He laid his hand gently back on the bed and left the room. He turned to Faelynn and watched her for a long moment before saying, "How can I ever repay you for saving my life. If you hadn't called Jackie to find me I don't know how much longer I could have lasted." He reached for her hand and squeezed it, "We have a lot to talk about, once I get out of here. Will you have dinner with me so we can talk?" She nodded her head, *yes*. She walked out the door as the tears slipped down her cheek.

Kurt had waited for her and they walked back to their grandmother's room. She turned to Kurt, "When do you get off work?" He looked at his watch. "Looks like I'm off now. Let me get downstairs and wash up and sign out. I'll meet you at the front door you know where." They both smiled and he left. Faelynn looked at her grandmother, "So what do you think of my brother, grandmother?" Her grandmother looked at her with such pride, "I'm so glad you're home to take over handling everything. I haven't been very good at that sort of thing. Earl handled everything before he died and Jack did later and then there was no one so I put everything in boxes or containers and it waited for you to return home to do it." She put her arm around her grandmother, "Oh good, does that mean I can go through all that stuff in the shed?" her grandmother laughed, "Oh, please be my guest." They hugged and Faelynn told her, "We're going to the court house to get some things done today and I want to get the house signed over to him." Her grandmother patted her hand, "I think you did the right thing. I truly love him and want him in our family. I didn't know your father had even finalized the adoption. I knew he was looking at several more children but I had no idea he had already taken one." With a hug and a kiss Faelynn left her grandmother's room and walked out the front door to see her brother waiting for her.

She met Kurt at the bench and they headed off to the attorney's office. When they got there again the room was filled with people. She signed them in and sat back down. They both looked around the room and at each other. She didn't recognize any of the people because it looked like a whole new group. The secretary came out to call them inside and she looked at Kurt and smiled as if to say, *see these people are here for display.* They were seated in front of the attorney and waited for him to hang up his phone. He picked up their folder, which was growing larger by the minute. He looked at his clients and smiled broadly, "I have good news about the four other investment accounts that you gave me. It looks like the money from them is being deposited in a bank in New York. They are industrial accounts and all bear your parent's names. I have contacted the investment firm he used to purchase them and they will be frozen until I contact him back." He then looked at Faelynn, "Do you want to hear the amount?" Faelynn looked at Kurt, "Do you want to know how much is in the account?" his reply was, "Can my heart take it?"

She laughed and turned to the attorney who was patiently waiting, "Yes." He cleared his throat before giving them what they sought. "You are undoubtedly one of the richest families in the entire nation and especially the state of Georgia. These accounts hold three hundred fifty eight million dollars and a bit of change here and there." Faelynn and Kurt sat there very numb from shock. He wiped his hand over his face but his hand shook so bad he had to hold it down on the chair. The secretary came in with refreshments and handed them each coffee. They finally recovered and stared at the attorney. The attorney continued, "The reason he had the accounts in New York is because they are very high risk roll over accounts and your father could have lost it all at the end of any day when the stock market closed. I felt with so much money involved you should make any decision as to whether you wanted it left there to be risked or pulled out into a safer stock. I have to admire your father's investment strategy he was a genius. He invested in new stock when it first came out and when it hit the top he pulled it out and reinvested in new technology stock. A genius, that's what he was. Now a decision has to be made on the stocks, I'm sure you don't want to keep gambling with them on the market. Do you want the funds transferred or invested into another stock that is a lower yield but not so apt to decline rapidly as the ones now."

Faelynn looked at Kurt, "Sister of mine you have done a great job so far and I defer to any decision you make. After all you're older than me." She gave him a scrunched up face and then smiled. "We want most of the money pulled from the high risk stocks. Only leave about five hundred thousand in the high-risk account, after all the money did well for fifteen years. Then I will open a general account for our charities, which half the money will go there. Then the balance will be divided and put into each of our trust accounts. Is that all right with you brother? He couldn't speak because he knew if he did he would break down and cry. *Our Charities*, she knew he wanted to help orphaned children and so did she. This would give them the working capital they needed to put some good programs together for them. He took her hand in his and replied, "You know me well, don't you?" She smiled at him as she replied, "As you know me?"

The secretary had written down their instructions and removed the tray, leaving them along again with the attorney. Faelynn reached for her purse saying, "There are a few other things that we need to have done. One is to have Kurt's name changed to the family name, after all his adoption was completed. He should have the right to use the family name. The attorney agreed and had Kurt sign a few papers and his Secretary typed them up while they were still in his office. She looked at the attorney and said, "There is one more job for your private investigator." She reached into her purse and pulled out the pictures with the names on the back and handed them to him. She watched as he looked at the photos, "These are the other children that my father was going to adopt. I would like a report on each one as to where they are? Where they work and how their life has been."

She reached into her brief case and pulled out their two folders and handed them to the attorney. "I'd like a report on these two families. I want to know how many children there were and where each one is. I know there is a lot of information to collect but he can hire several men to help him and I'll pay for it. Tell him not to miss one detail either. Can you make copies of these I want them back.

There is one more thing that I would like for you to do and that is to send a letter to the address in the folders, the adoption agency, letting them know you're representing us and that they will be put on a monthly allowance of five thousand dollars to start. The conditions that they will receive this money are these, they will have monthly inspections by the health department and social services who will require signed documents as to their findings and will be audited every six months to be sure the money is being put into the orphanage instead of his pocket. The man who runs it is listed on the papers also. I think he spends the money donated to the orphanage on antiques for his office and home and doesn't put too much toward the care of the children. I want a closed end agreement to make sure he has to report every dime on his audit."

The secretary finished with her short hand and walked into the other room to get it typed up. Faelynn stood and reached out her hand to shake the attorney's hand. "You have been doing an excellent job taking care of things that I feel are very important. I want you to know I appreciate it. He smiled at her still holding her hand in his, "It's my pleasure and I'll be in touch when we have other news to discuss and of course copies of everything we discussed will be sent over to you." She handed him another check and he smiled.

When they got back to the car Kurt turned to her with a look of admiration, "You know Faelynn, when I first saw you I thought you to be a sweet and gentle girl but after that visit to the attorney I now find my sister is a real tough cookie." She hit him on the arm, "I am still a sweet gentle girl." They both laughed and got back into the car. She looked at Kurt as he started the car and adjusted his mirror, "No sense in changing the property until your name change is done. Then it will be signed over properly. By the way, when's the wedding?" Kurt blushed a little and became tongue tied, "I don't know, Diane hasn't told me yet." Faelynn laughed, "Tell her if she needs any help to let me know and I'd be glad to do anything to help her."

Kurt gave a serious face, "Did you know, she has no parents, both of them are dead. He lost her dad to cancer and her mom wilted away after he died." Faelynn turned and put her arm on his shoulder and patted it, "Oh, I'm so sorry Kurt. I didn't know. It must have been a terrifying time for her losing them close to the same time." He shook his head and replied, "Yeah, we talked about it when I showed her the house. She loved it and especially the dishes; she did just like we did. She walked around touching everything."

Faelynn changed the subject by saying," We need to be thinking what we're going to do with the other kids dad was going to adopt. How much are we going to share with them and how we will handle it?" Kurt thought for a minute before replying, "I think we should look them over good to be sure they're on the up and up before telling them who we are and how we came to know them." Faelynn totally agreed, "Yes, that is a good idea to be around them a little before we identify ourselves. See brother you're coming up with some good solid ideas now. I guess we'd better get back to the hospital and take grandmother home or she will think we abandoned her."

CHAPTER 12

They rode in silence for a while then Kurt snapped his fingers, "Hey, let's stop by the Auto mall. I do really need a new car?" and he looked at her beat-up car and said, "So do you." So back to the Auto mall they went. Kurt's miser mode kicked again, "I think I know what kind of car I want, but it may cost too much to buy. I might just look today." Faelynn laughed, "Do you think there's a cure for being a tightwad?" Then, they both laughed. A salesman met them at the door and inquired how he could help them. She looked at her brother, "What kind of car was that Kurt?" He looked at her and the salesman and replied, "A BMW." She turned to the salesman and saw him smacking his lips at that commission. She took her brother's hand, "Lead us to them."

The salesman showed them ten models from which to choose. Kurt looked them over and over and over. She finally became angry at his indecision, "Enough of the sampling just chose one brother." He grinned at her and walked over to one, "Okay, this one time I'll let you win." He chose the red one with the white convertible top. The salesman led them to his office to fill out the paperwork. He talked the entire time and it about drove Faelynn crazy. She stood up rubbing her temples, "This is our attorney's name get your information from him. I'll take one just like his except in white. Have the red one delivered to the hospital fourth floor nurses station and have the other one delivered here, and handed him a card with her address on it. This is our banker he can give you a cashier's check for both of them. Don't make us wait too long or we'll be looking for them somewhere else."

They got up and left the establishment. Faelynn was still rubbing her temple, "I have a migraine. I'm going home to bed for a while. I'll call you when it goes away and you can bring grandmother home." You can drop me off and take the car with you. He looked concerned with her sudden headache. "Are you alright sis?" She rubbed at her temples again, "I think it is just getting all the business handled. I didn't realize how stressed It was trying to get father's affairs in order." He drove her home and made sure she was safely inside before he left. He was worried about her because she was always so peppy and had never feigned a headache.

She walked upstairs and went to her room and lay down. She fell asleep quickly. She awoke to a loud noise downstairs but was too sleepy to realize what it had been. The phone rang and she answered it, "Hello." The person on the other end was Officer Chastain. He said, "Miss Myers, Steven Smith has escaped county jail early this morning when the laundry truck was here to take the laundry out. I knew he had been harassing you and wanted to warn you to lock your doors and screens." She quickly walked to the bedroom door and locked it. She whispered, "It is too late, I think he is downstairs now. I just heard a loud noise there it probably was the back door." The officer said, "I have ordered two cars out to your place now it shouldn't be more than ten minutes. Go into your bathroom and lock that door too. It will deter him a little longer so that the patrol cars will get there in time. Hurry, if you have a cell phone call your neighbors so that they can get there too. Make sure they don't attempt to go after him." She agreed and picked up her cell phone and stepped inside and locked her bathroom door. She dialed Jackie and her neighbor across the street. They both arrived at the house in no time. Mr. Jones laid on his horn to get the neighbors attention. They could use any help that could get there.

Jackie drew his gun and stepped through the back door. He saw Steven in the office tearing files out of a drawer looking for something. He pointed the gun and told him, "Get your hands up, now." Steven looked at him and laughed, "You won't shoot me. I could take that gun away from you in a heartbeat." Jackie held it still as he ordered Steven out the door. They were in the back yard when the two officers arrived. They ran up to Steven and took his hands to his back to cuff him. Steven suddenly flung the officers back from him in a rage and started running for the car. The officers yelled, "Halt, Halt, but Steven kept on running. The one officer fired and hit him in the leg. Steven was all red in the face and angry and ran back toward the police officer that had shot him. He started yelling, "I'm not going back to that animal house. It's all her fault I was put there in the first place. She deserves to die for it too." He lunged at the officer with his hands up as if he was going to claw him and the officer pulled the trigger again. Steven crumpled to the ground and didn't move. The officer called for an ambulance and a detective. Anytime there was a death by an officer a detective had to investigate it. Jackie ran up the steps calling for Faelynn. She opened the door and he hugged her. "You don't know how lucky you are because he had intended on killing you because he blamed his problems on you."

She released him, "Did the police get him then? "Jackie didn't say anything right away and Faelynn looked at him, "Jackie?" Jackie looked at her white face and wide eyes, "Faelynn, he isn't going to bother you ever again, he's dead."

She began to get dizzy and leaned into him. He steadied her but kept a firm arm around her, "It was for the best, he threatened kill you, and who knows one day he might have succeeded. It's over now for good." Faelynn looked at Jackie thinking of how this news would upset Richard, "Please don't mention this to Richard. He'll be so worried. I want him to concentrate on getting well." He nodded and promised, "I won't, I promise. But if you need me you'll call won't you?" She gave him another hug, "Of course." He walked back down stairs to see if the police needed him any further and he then drove back to his home. The police thanked Mr. Jones and he returned to his home. She came down to the living room and looked around the office and kitchen. There was that door again. She might as well build a revolving door and it would not have to be broken down again.

She walked into the office to see files and folders torn out and lying on the floor, chair and desktop. She picked up the files from the floor and looked at them. They were household bills and expenses for the house. She picked the two from the chair and those were inventories of father's holdings. The one on the top of the desk is the one that concerned her and it was of the children her father and mother had considering adopting. What could he possibly want with that file? The police came in after the ambulance picked up the body and told her that they would be leaving. They said, "Since Jackie is sending someone over to fix the door again and some dirt has been spread out on the drive way, there wasn't anything else they could do there. So, they were going back to the station to fill out their reports. Officer Chastain handed her a card, "Can you call Detective Reeves in a few days? He will need to talk to you." She agreed and they left her yard. She still looked bewildered at the picture and read their names over and over trying to make a connection to Steven Smith. She took the two girls pictures and put them back inside the folder. She sat looking at the two boys faces. Did their eyes look different did their hair or face shape look familiar. She sighed and had to admit that nothing caught her attention.

She stood up and was walking out the door when the phone rang. She reached for it and said, "Hello." It was Kurt on the other end. He asked, "Are you feeling better? Did you get rid of the headache?" She thought for a minute about how her grandmother would react to finding a broken door, but she said, "Yes, it is gone. Are you bringing grandmother home? I must tell you that Steven Smith broke into the house again and threatened to kill me. Oh, that strong door at the back of the house is broken again. You might want to let her know about it before she sees it. The police shot Steven so he won't be bothering me anymore. But Kurt, He insisted that I owed him something. He pulled the adoption file out of the desk and had it on the table. There were two boys that father was looking at, do you think he could have been one?" Kurt was at a complete loss, "Why would he want to kill you if our father had wanted to adopt him. How would he have known, he would have been too young to know. Someone would have had to tell him that information."

She knew Kurt had been right and that someone would have told him that father had wanted to adopt him for him to continue to show up here. Maybe he felt that he should have been adopted before Kurt. Or he resented the family because they hadn't adopted him. It was so bizarre to the point of not making any sense at all. "Well I guess we will just have to wait until the attorney gets the bios on each of them before we'll know for sure. See you in a little while. I'll fix some sandwiches and we can all have lunch together." She hung up the phone and started to pick up the folders and put them back into the file. She looked through the files quickly to make sure they were all there. She looked under the desk and found one kicked back under the desk. She bent down to get it and as she looked at it the file name said, Steven Smith. My goodness what was this about? She opened the file and saw the first date of the folder was dated almost twenty-five years ago. She didn't have time to read the file now because Kurt was on his way so she tucked it into her briefcase for reading later.

She had put the folder away but it was still on her mind. Why would her grandmother have a file on him? Now she was getting curious to read it, but definitely alone. She fixed a few sandwiches and put out a few cookies she had picked up. She had some fresh fruit she set on the table, strawberries and cantaloupe. She put the plates and glasses on the table along with the silverware. She heard the car drive into the yard and went out to greet them. She gave her grandmother a big hug and walked her inside followed by Kurt and Diane. She looked back at them and smiled, "Lunch is on the table." They walked into the dining room and she helped her grandmother into her chair. Her grandmother sat at the table with her hands folded together. "Kurt was telling me you had a little trouble with some man who wanted to work on the house."

Faelynn looked at her grandmother and thought how best to handle this without upsetting her. "Yes, he was insistent about working for us but I found him too aggressive and decided not to give him the job, so he got mad at me and broke into the house a time or two. But it is all taken care of and Jackie is coming over today to fix the door for us."

She didn't know how other to explain it without upsetting her elderly grandmother and she wasn't about to do that. Her grandmother was looking around the room and noticed the many changes. "I see you have been remodeling this old place. I would like to see it all after we eat." Faelynn looked at her and patted her hand, "One house tour coming right up after lunch." They all laughed together. It seemed right now to Faelynn to have people in the house laughing together. It was nice to be able to see that happen before something happened to her grandmother.

She took a bite of her sandwich and looked at Kurt, "How is your patient doing? Is there much improvement?" He nodded and finished chewing the bite of his sandwich, "A great deal actually. It is as if he is willing himself well. He still asks for you." Faelynn thought how easy it would be to go to him but it wouldn't be right. He would have to come to her and apologize for his actions before they could talk again. "He needs this time to heal and not be bothered with company. His family is there they will care for him." Kurt didn't say anything else about it but knew that she had been deeply hurt by Richard's mistrust.

After lunch they walked into the living room and grandmother did a lot of pleasing sighs, "Faelynn, it is beautiful. It looks like it did when I first came to this house. Thank you for doing this for me" They walked up the stairs to her room and she opened the door and stood very still.

Her eyes took in all the beautiful old antiques all polished up and the beautiful hand crocheted doilies that lay on the refurbished furniture. The curtains matched the pattern in the doilies. The pictures hanging on the wall brought tears to her eyes. They were so beautiful and looked so elegant hanging there. They had moved her bed so she could see the side yard and the road. It looked much better there. She turned to her granddaughter as a tear trickled down her cheek, "Faelynn, you have did a wonderful job remodeling the house. It looks perfect. It looks as good as when I arrived and I was carried across this very threshold by Earl, I sighed and whispered, I'm home."

She hugged her grandmother, "I'm glad you like it. I thought it might cheer you up." Her grandmother put her hands on her cheeks exclaiming, "That it surely did, it is again a show place." They walked back down the stairs to the living room and sat around talking. The phone rang and she answered, "Hello." It was the car dealer, Miss Myers; I sent the car to the hospital but couldn't find Kurt. They told me that he was at his grandmother's house, so I sent both cars there. Is that all right?" She laughed because she was pleasantly surprised, "Yes, that is fine." She then hung up the phone. She laughed out loud and looked at Kurt. She heard a horn and looked out the window. "There's something in the driveway for you, brother." He jumped up and ran outside. There in the yard were two matching cars but for different colors. Diane joined him and was looking at the cars. He grabbed her hand and pointed, "The red one is ours." Diane put her hand over her heart as if to check to see if it was still beating. "You bought a car? You really bought a car?" Diane was speechless.

Faelynn and her grandmother walked outside to see Diane and Kurt getting in their car. He yelled to them, "I'll be back in a while; I'm taking it for a spin." They waved as he pulled out of the drive way and put the top down. Diane sat so close to him he couldn't have shifted if he needed to. Good thing it was an automatic. Her grandmother looked at her and grinned, "You bought a car? You really bought a car? I thought you were too thrifty to buy a new car." Faelynn hugged her grandmother, "I was surprised that Kurt agreed to get the cars. I felt it was time to spend a little money on something more dependable than our old cars." She wondered where Kurt got his thriftiness from, but she already knew. It had been the same for her, having to penny pinch to scrape by a living because she wouldn't touch a penny of her trust fund except for her education. Then they both laughed. Her grandmother patted her arm, with a choked voice she whispered, "Your grandfather and your father would be so proud of you."

She took her grandmother's arm and walked back into the house. They spent the rest of the afternoon talking about their ever-growing family. Her grandmother looked at her with kindness and love, "Your responsible for bring happiness back to this house. I'm so happy to see it here again." Faelynn didn't say anything just sat there in deep thought. What would her grandmother think if she told her about the other kids? She decided to chance it. She took a deep breath and began her questions. "Grandmother, did you know Steven Smith or ever have any work done by him on the house?" She thought for a minute before replying, "No, I have never met him before. Why?" She didn't want to upset her grandmother but at the same time she needed to know if they had previously had any contact with him. She asked another question. "Do you know if Grandfather Earl knew him or let him work here? Her grandmother thought again and said, "No, Dear, I don't think either of us knew him." Faelynn tapped her cheek with her finger, "I've been racking my brain trying to figure out why he would think that our family owed him. He kept saying that to me. It just really didn't make any sense and I though perhaps you might know the answer."

Her grandmother stood abruptly, "I think I'm going to lie down for a while. I don't want to overdo myself the first day home." Faelynn stood and went to her side, "Do you need some help?" Her grandmother shook her head and replied, "No, I'll be down later." Faelynn walked into the kitchen to do up the dishes that had been left from lunch. After she had put them into the drainer to dry, she remembered the file she had stuck in her briefcase. She retrieved it and went back to the living room and sat in one of the overstuffed chairs. She opened it to read. She had gotten to the second page before she muttered, *oh my god.*

She read it again to be sure her mind wasn't playing tricks on her. It was a birth certificate attached to a letter from a Ramona Smith. It was addressed to Grandfather Earl at the home address. The letter read, My Dear Darling Earl, I hate to have to write to tell you that I have recently given birth to a son. I have named him Steven. Here is a copy of his birth certificate and it names you as his father. I hope you realize that I would not try to pawn another man's baby off as yours.

Since I can no longer work I had hoped that you might help me out until I can get back on my feet and get back to work. It would only be a temporary arrangement if you can see it in your heart to help me. I do hope to see you again if you get back to Austin, Texas on another buying trip. I wouldn't have known how to find you but that nice man you were acquainted with happened to have you name and address and gave it to me. I hope to hear from you soon because I have used most my savings and do not know where to go from here.

Please write me back as quickly as possible, I still love you, Your Ramona. Faelynn turned the letter over and looked at the envelope and saw it was dated March of 1950. She looked at the letter again to be sure she wasn't dreaming. She looked at the other sheet in the folder and it showed where grandfather Earl had sent money to her to support the child. He had sent her at least a hundred dollars a month for his support. Well, I guess it answers the question of why Steven thought our family owed him something. There was another letter about two years later where she sent a picture of the baby. Faelynn studied it for a while and it did look like her father a little.

He had been looking for this file and had he found it he probably would have gone public with the information and embarrassed her grandmother. She didn't believe that her grandmother knew of her grandfather Earl's affair. Even if she did, she wouldn't have talked about it. The question now was what, was she going to do with it. Destroying it would wipe it from our family forever. Then again if another member of his family came forward it would prove that grandfather provided for him growing up. She weighed the pros and cons and decided to keep the file. She would put it in a safe place in case she needed it. Should, she never need it then she will destroy it after ten years is up.

Now knowing that grandfather Earl had been having an affair with another woman she wondered about her own father. Would he have had an affair on his wife? They seemed so devoted to each other. She could only speculate but probably not. They acted like newlyweds most of the time.

Her phone rang and she answered, "Hello." A man said in a whispered voice, "Hello Darling." She recognized Richard's voice. Her breath caught in her throat and her chest tightened. "Hello Richard, How are you feeling?" He had to talk with effort and she knew he was in a lot of pain yet. "Better now, that I have heard your voice again." She didn't know what to say to him. She didn't want to encourage him if he would never trust her. She couldn't live like that nor did she want to. She asked him about his hospital arrangements, "Have they moved you to a regular room? Are they letting you have visitors now?" He struggled to reply, "Yes, I'm in a room now but they are limiting my visits still. Can you come to see me?"

She hesitated a minute, but he sensed she was going to say no, so he said, "Please, Faelynn, we need to talk."

She responded, "Richard, I'm not certain that talking right now is going to do anything but complicate the problem. I will stop by there for a few minutes and no more. You need your rest and you need to heal. You have suffered a lot of damage from your accident. You need your family around you at this time in your life. They are a great deal of support." He didn't say anything else and she hung up the phone. She went upstairs and freshened up and picked up her purse. The file she was looking at was tucked back into her briefcase and locked. She went out to her new car and started it up. She drove down to the hospital. She admired the beauty and smoothness of her new car as she drove into the hospital parking lot. She went to the floor that Richard had given her. There were a few of his family there so she checked in with the nurse's station and went to sit with them. Jackie and Annette greeted her. She explained her presence there, "Richard called me and asked me to come down here. I'm not sure what he wants. Do you have any idea? Annette looked at Jackie, "He wants to apologize to you. I told him about Kurt being your brother and I think now he is embarrassed that he didn't ask you about it before running off like a spoiled child." Jackie tried to stick up for him but Annette gave him a sympathetic look and he just hung his head. The nurse came out into the waiting room and asked for Faelynn. She stood up but wasn't sure if she wanted to follow the nurse or walk out the door. Even though she still cared about him she could not forgive him for how he has treated her. She followed the nurse inside only because she had promised to come see him. She walked over to his bed and stood there looking at him. He was attached to several tubes and bottles. He reached for her hand and pulled it closer to his chest. He looked at her face and knew he had put that look there. She was hurt and he had done it again, all because of his jealousy. He spoke in a soft voice, "It is good to see you again, and I have missed you. When I was lying out there in the car on that embankment you're the only one I thought of day after day. You're the only one that heard me calling for help. I can't ever repay you for my life."

Faelynn was careful about what she said; she didn't want to make him think she felt anything for him because now she wasn't sure she did. He had questioned her faithfulness and her honesty and that was hard to deal with, especially from a man you once loved. "I'm glad you're doing better. I hope you continue to heal. It's a long journey and will take a long time for you to get back to normal. Has Alexandria come to see you yet?" Richard knew he'd done a lot of damage to her this time. She might not even care for him anymore after he had assumed she was having an affair with another man. How could he have been so stupid? He had a lot to make up for, if she would ever give him the chance.

Faelynn watched as a change came over his face, "Would you like for me to get you a book to read while you're recuperating? They have some good books out now that might interest you." She was being polite, their relationship and been put back to square one. Polite after all they had meant to each other. He held her hand tight in his and prayed she would answer his question. "Faelynn, I know I have really messed our relationship up this time but will you promise to come and see me while I'm here so we can talk. We need to talk to each other. I want us to get back to our comfortable place where we were before I became a total idiot. Can we please talk a little every day?"

She pulled her hand back and put it in her pocket. She didn't know if they could ever reach that plateau again. It had been fragile and sacred ground that had been filled with mistrust and anger. "I'm not sure it is a good idea to do that Richard. I think you need to heal before even going into another relationship. You need some time to think about the mistakes that were made and how to avoid them in the future. To be honest, I'm not sure I'm ready to go back there either. I must go now. Take care of yourself and get lots of rest so you can heal." She walked out the door and didn't stop until she got outside to her car where she stood and trembled. She slid into her car and put both hands over her face and cried.

She had loved Richard, could she again? The delicate love she had for him had been shattered by mistrust. Mistrust and Jealousy is the root that destroys love along with people's lives. Maybe she should let it go as it is. She didn't want to hurt as bad as she did when she fled this place the first time to lick her wounds in Oregon. *That is it!* She needed to get away for a while and let Richard heal of his wounds and she could figure out what she wanted to do herself. That is a good idea. She would have Kurt and Diane stay at the house with grandmother. Yes, that would be perfect. She started her car and drove to the grocery store and then to the bank to draw out some money. Then she returned to her home. She would rent a beach house and spend a week or two just taking in some rest and relaxation of her own.

She carried the groceries into the house, and saw her grandmother in the living room reading. She put the groceries away and went to join her grandmother. She looked at her grandmother and seemed please that she had recovered so quickly. "Grandmother, I'm going to be going on a short vacation to relax some. I've been having some headaches and I think it is from trying so hard to get father's affairs in order. I'm going to call Kurt and Diane to see if they wouldn't mind staying here for a week or so with you. I hope you don't mind it's just that I've been working for the last two months with no break. I'm going to tell you where I am going but I would appreciate your not telling anyone. Can I count on you for that?" Her grandmother spoke up, "I think it's a good idea. I think you deserve some rest after all you have taken over the running of the family and its finances. Go with my blessing and rest. Come back all vibrant as you were before, and Faelynn, I won't break my promise to you because I know this is an important decision you're going to be making. Bless you my child. She hugged her granddaughter and kissed her on the cheek. Take all the time you need."

Faelynn called Kurt and talked to him about it and he agreed that she needed some rest and time to think. He was happy that she had made a decision for her welfare. "We'll be more than happy to stay with grandmother. We'll move into the spare bedroom tonight. It will give grandmother a chance to get to know Diane better too. We have our license to get married now it is just setting the date. We want to get the rings this weekend when I'm off. Let me see did I leave anything out?" He laughed and she laughed with him, he was so funny and lifted her spirits. She did tell him, "Oh, the attorney will call us and make an appointment when he gets the reports about the other kids. Your court date will be soon to have your name change done. Remind me to tell you a family secret when I get back. You'll be amazed. Now, that should keep you wondering for a week or so. I have to call the airline to get a ticket. I want to leave tomorrow morning. Thanks Kurt for doing this for me. I do appreciate it." Kurt knew she needed this time alone to do some thinking. With all the problems she has dealt with, it was important to give this to her. He was pleased. "I'll see you later tonight then. Love you lots." Then the phone went dead.

She called the airport and got her reservation and called the motel she stayed at in Oregon when she went to the beach. Everything was set for early tomorrow morning. She went to her room and packed a bag for her trip. She could buy some more clothes if she needed them there. She may stay longer than she had planned once she gets there. That night Kurt and Diane moved into the spare bedroom. The girls fixed supper and enjoyed each other's company. They cooked small steaks and a baked potato with a salad. It was good to have family around again. Kurt and Diane took her to the airport early the next morning. They sat around in the airport lounge talking until they called her flight. There were hugs and kisses around then she walked down the ramp into the plane. The plane taxied onto the runway as Kurt and Diane watched, until it was in the air, before heading for their car and the hospital.

CHAPTER 13

It was early evening when her plane landed in Portland, Oregon and taxied onto the runway. Its doors opened for the crowds to evacuate the plane. There was chatter all around her but she was not in a chatting mood.

She drove her rented car to her hotel and registered for the night. She called her two friends and they met her in the lobby for dinner. They chatted and laughed for a long time. She told them she was driving to the beach tomorrow to spend a week walking the beach. She explained that she had been handling the family problems and finances and just needed a few days to herself. They were jealous because that was their favorite thing to do. They had a scrumptious meal and she enjoyed their company and didn't realize how much she missed them.

She bid them farewell and told them she would be leaving early the next morning for the ocean. She had rented the car at the airport and would return it when she caught her flight back to Georgia. She left a wakeup call for four in the morning so she could get a good start. She loaded her bag into the car and drove west on the main road to Tillamook, Oregon. She arrived there in a few hours and registered at the little Sand Dune Motel. It was nice and clean and close to town and it had a coffee pot in the room. It was within walking distance to many stores and restaurants. The little motel was perfect it was just perfect.

She unpacked her bag and changed to something comfortable and walked the beach. She watched the waves come in and the seagull's meet them, looking for fresh fish for their lunch. The sun was out and the breeze drifted past her. Maybe, she should have stayed here; it was so peaceful and quiet. There was nothing to do but watch the waves and she sure loved to do that. She walked about a half mile up the beach and saw a little food stand. She stopped and had a hot dog and fries for lunch with a soda pop. She looked around the little town and thought how happy these people were just to have the ocean at their backs. She meandered through the shops and picked up a few pieces of fruit, juice and snacks in case she wanted something later that night.

She walked to the beach and started her trek back to the motel. She walked and walked and didn't see but one other person on the beach. By the time she got back to the motel the sun was setting over the water. She borrowed a chair from her room and went out back of the motel to watch it. It was such a dramatic setting when the colors of the sky floated from one side of the sky to the other changing colors as it went. It was a beautiful thing to see. It started to get dark and she went into her room. She turned her television on to watch the local news. It gave all the latest news around the country and then the local news and the weather followed. She knew from experience that the conditions on the ocean could go from warm and sunny one day to thunderstorms and heavy rain the next. She had brought several books to read in case she got stuck in the room.

She tried not to think about Richard but she couldn't help it. It was almost like the first time she came here, to forget him. It didn't work then and it won't work now. So the next best thing to do is to relax and enjoy the vacation. The next morning, she walked back to the little town and found her a beach towel a short robe and some sunglasses. She walked back again to the motel and took her beach towel and a bottle of water out of the mini fridge and walked down to the water. Since the tourist season had passed she had the beach pretty much to herself. Occasionally, she would see a couple or some kids walking on the beach but not too many people were around now. She didn't care because she was still enjoying herself being alone. She had picked up a paper to see what was going on in town and for some coupons on special deals. It said there was an art show coming to the area in the next week maybe she would go to it. That should be fun. The sky began to change and dark clouds rolled in above her. She folded the paper and picked up her towel and walked back toward the motel. Suddenly, she heard thunder and the lightening began. She was sure the news didn't say anything about a storm coming. She started to run for her room when she felt big plops of rain hitting her. She reached the shelter of the covered awning just as the bottom fell out of the sky and the rains came down fast.

She opened her room and went inside turning the light on as she came in. She locked the door and headed for the shower. She toweled her hair dry as she came into the room to listen to the news. She walked to the chair and sat down while looking through the assortment of books she had brought with her. She found a mystery and laid it by the chair. She peeked outside at the rain that was coming down in sheets. She wondered how long it would last. Surely, it couldn't be too much longer. If it was going to do this the whole time she was here then she could go back home to the sunshine.

The rain did let up and she enjoyed the beach once more. Every day, she could be found sitting out in the sunshine watching the waves and the seagulls. She discovered that she could take some bread and break it into small pieces and when she threw it into the air the seagulls would grab it in flight. They hovered above her each day looking for their treat. She was beginning to relax and enjoy her time there. She walked and walked for miles up and down the beach. She picked up seashells and found a coin or two in the sand. The days drifted into weeks and she soon realized she had been there a month. The weather was beginning to get chillier and she realized it was time to go home. She knew the winter months in the northeast and northwest could be deadly. She called the airport and made her reservations to fly to Atlanta and packed her bags. Early the next morning she checked out of the motel and put her bag into the car. She drove back to Portland and turned in the car and caught the plane back to Georgia.

She knew nothing had changed but she did relax and it gave her plenty of time to think. Can people make mistakes and not do it again? Can you love someone and not love him, at the same time? Could she live with Richard and have him trust her or her trust him. They had a lot of history together but most of it hurt. Was her love strong enough or was his? Those were tough questions. But she still needed to know if he truly could love and trust her. She had no place in her life for jealously or mistrust. Those seemed to be the two big issues.

She felt that Richard and she could get along and there was nothing major that they had to argue about, just the two evils of the world. Could she live without him? What if they couldn't work out their problems and had to stay apart. Could they live in the same town? She was beginning to get the headache again. She rubbed her temples and laid her head back on the seat. She drifted off to sleep and was awaken by a stewardess telling her, they were in Atlanta. She looked at her watch and found that the time had passed while she slept. She picked up her one piece of luggage and walked outside to hail a cab. She found one and gave them the address in Covington. They arrived safely and she paid the cabbie and took her luggage to the door. The house seemed quiet as she opened the door and went inside. She locked the door and turned on the light. She called to her grandmother and her brother Kurt but no one answered. She cut the light on in the living room and almost screamed. She saw a man sitting on the sofa just staring into the darkness. She yelled, "What the heck are you doing here trying to give me a heart attack?" Richard turned to look at her and stood up with the help of a cane. She watched him as he hobbled over to her. She repeated her question. "What are you doing here?" He answered it with his soft lips on hers. "I came here because I love you and I'm so sorry I ever doubted our love. You have always been the only woman I have ever loved and will ever love. Life isn't worth living if you're not in it. I'm begging you to give us a new start. I promise I won't mess it up again. Faelynn you are my heart and soul without you I am nothing but a shell of a man. I don't want to have to exist in life I want to live it with you. I want to have children with you. I'll wait forever if you promise to marry me."

She looked into his eyes and saw the love he offered her. She knew that she had always loved him and what is important in life if we can't share it with the one we love. He stood there in front of her with his arms open. She could walk into them or walk away. If she walked away she would never find a love such as Richard's again. Then she realized there was no choice. She walked into his arms and he wrapped them around her. She had come home. Home to where her heart lived.

They stood holding each other for the longest time. He finally broke the contact to put his hand under her chin and raise her face to his for a deep kiss. He tightened his hold on her until they were almost one body. He stepped back but held her with his arm. He reached into his pocket and brought out a black box and opened it for her to see a beautiful sparkling diamond ring. He watched her face to see if she truly loved him, "I love you with all my heart and soul. Will you marry me and allow me to spend my life with you?" The tears slid down her face as she looked up into his loving face, "Yes, I would love to spend my life with you. There has never been anyone else for me but you." He took the ring and placed it on her finger and kissed her again. They sat back down on the couch and talked about what kind of wedding she wanted and when they should get married and where. They decided to get married soon and Faelynn suggested, "I would like to have a small church wedding and have a reception on the grounds." Richard didn't have a problem with that as long as it was soon, very soon.

CHAPTER 14

Faelynn and Kurt revisited the attorney. She had given him five pictures two boys and three girls. They arrived to a room full of people. After signing in they walked back to their chairs and watched the other people in the room. Again, the receptionist came to the door and called them first. Now, they looked at each other with knowing thoughts. That lawyer had to be paying those people to sit in his office all day to make him look busy. They both chuckled. They were sitting in front of the attorney again watching him shuffle the folders around. He stopped and looked at both of them with a smile on his face.

He cleared his throat and started to speak. "Well, it seems we have a lot to talk about today. We will cover the history of the five orphans your parents were thinking of adopting. The first one is Anthony Hall. He was adopted from the home within two months after being delivered there by his mother. Actually, he was adopted right after the orphanage had sent his picture on to your father, so he would have already been adopted by the time your father would have left for his honeymoon. I would not count him because he would have already been placed." He looked at Faelynn and Kurt for a response.

They looked at each other and Faelynn said, "Well, that is true he wouldn't have been available for adoption by our parents so, 'yes,' I think we can count him out. Don't you agree Kurt?" Kurt thought for a minute then asked, "So, how is Anthony Hall doing now? Is he able to make ends meet and does he have a family?"

The attorney picked up the folder and handed it to Kurt. Kurt looked through it and saw that the man was a farmer with ten kids and a large farm. His wife was still living and they had a full range farm that was productive and well set financially. He smiled and laid it back on the table. "I agree that we can count Anthony out." The attorney smiled and opened another folder. He flipped up a page and read off the name. "This is Brenda Cashley; she owns a beauty salon in Alabama and was adopted six months after being at the orphanage. Her beauty shop is located in Mobile, Alabama and she is doing quite well for herself. She is married with two children, a boy and a girl. Her husband is in the military and they own their own home and according to the neighbors and her business associates they are a very happily married couple. Kurt and Faelynn looked at each other and both said in unison, "We agree, we can count her out."

The attorney picked up another folder and flipped the page to read the name. "This one is Lois Moon; she is a secretary for a major bottling company and has been in her position since she was eighteen years old. She makes good money and has benefits with savings accounts. She was married twice with no children. Her last husband passed away a few years back leaving her with a handsome insurance policy but now she is presently dating one of the officers of the corporation and some of her close friends say it is going to be a permanent position because they're talking marriage." He looked at Faelynn and Kurt and they both agreed again that she was financially set. "We think we can count Lois out."

Kurt looked at Faelynn, "Three down two do go." The attorney pulled another file and flipped the page to the name. "This one is Janie Walker; she is a social worker for the state of Alabama. She has been with them for three years, prior to that she; herself was receiving welfare for her and her four children. She barely makes ends meet and lives in a rundown place in the lower part of town." He looked at them and made his assessment. "Of the ones I have read, I think this one could use some help, but how to do it is the hard decision. If you walk right up to her and introduce yourself and give her the money then she could spend it all then come back for another handout. I'm not sure how you want to go about this but I'll hold the file until you make a decision." Both Kurt and Faelynn nodded their heads because they knew this had to be thought out first.

The attorney picked up the last folder and flipped the page to the name. "This is the last one and his name is Glenn Jones. He owns an automotive dealership and is doing quite well for himself. He has a large complex and many employees. I, personally, would think that he should be counted out." Kurt and Faelynn agreed and now it seems there is only one maybe two who could use their help. Kurt spoke first, "Can you hold Lois Moon's file along with Janie Walker's file for a few days so we can talk it over. The secretary position could change at any moment and if that happens then she could use some help too. Let us think on it for ten days and we'll be back in touch then. Kurt and Faelynn stood and shook hands with the attorney and left the room. They went to the local cafe and sat in the back talking about the two people that could use the help and how best they could help them.

The waitress came to take their order and they sat there waiting for it to be brought to them. After the waitress had left them, she cleared her throat and turned to Kurt. "I think I told you a while back that I had a family secret to tell you and that it would knock your socks off." He stared at her wondering what she could surprise him with now, "Okay, I'll bite, what's the family secret I haven't heard about?" She looked at him for a moment as if wondering if she was doing the right thing. She opened her purse and handed him the letter she found among her father's papers.

Kurt took the letter and read the postmark. It was from Austin, Texas. He muttered, "Hmmm..." he turned the envelope around and opened it. He read the letter and his eyes became enlarged the more he read. He looked at Faelynn, "Oh my goodness, does grandmother know?" Faelynn shook her head "*no,* the reason I am showing it to you is so that you will be able to see why Steven Smith came to the house. He was grandfather's illegitimate son. His mother is Ramona Smith and I think we should try to help her. I'm sure grandfather would want us to. Our father must have been sending her payments right up to his death. He had to know when he took over his mother's accounts. Had Steven came right out and told the truth then I would have tried to help him but he became threatening instead. I didn't know at the time, he was our uncle. No one knew of grandfather's affair until I discovered this letter. What do you think? Should we try to send her some money to help her out? It could be done anonymously by saying it was an insurance policy on Steven from his job, or something we could make up so she wouldn't be suspicious of our family."

Kurt looked at her for a moment then bowed his head shaking it. "You must have a forgiving heart, Faelynn; why else would you want to help the mother of the man who tried to kill you?" Faelynn shrugged her shoulder, "It wasn't her fault that her son became obsessed with our family and tried to harm us instead of just telling us the truth." Kurt shook his head, "Yes, you're right, he should have come right to the house and announced his claim on our family. Yes, I think we should definitely help her. She has no one now." Faelynn was relieved because she was going to do it anyway if he had disagreed. She felt now that she knew the truth; she should give his mother something.

They talked about the other person Janie Walker and her situation and how they could best help her. It sounded like she was needy on all fronts. Her home needed to be changed, her kids needed a nanny so she could have a life of her own and her job needed improvement, perhaps some more schooling to assist her in getting a better job. They were surprised to see that she still lived near the orphanage within a fifty-mile radius of it. They wondered why. Faelynn looked at Kurt, "Should we make another trip to Alabama to look her over?" He smiled as he drank his tea, "Well, of course, we can't help her if we don't see her in person." She smiled as he grinned, "Got any plans for the rest of the day? Maybe the four of us could go." Faelynn called Richard and Kurt called Diane and the four of them agreed to drive to Alabama. They met at the hospital and left Kurt's car there.

Richard drove for the first few hundred miles and then Kurt took over so they changed seats. When they crossed the Alabama line they started looking for a place to get a cup of coffee and a sandwich. They found a little restaurant in Saraland a little town just fifty miles from the orphanage. They walked inside and were seated at a booth by the window. On the way to Saraland, Kurt and Faelynn had explained to their partners what they were doing and why. They knew that they had to help the people that their parents had wanted to adopt. So they picked the ones that needed it the most.

They placed their order and sat talking until it arrived. They were hungry so everyone dug into their lunch. Richard took a drink of his tea; "I appreciate your inviting me on this outing. It's a great way to get acquainted with the family. I think it's a great idea that you both have about helping the other kids, your father was thinking of adopting. It is very generous too." Diane smiled at them; "I agree with Richard this is too much fun not to share it between us." She looked at Kurt then smiled, "This is where you run off to when you took some time off at the hospital?" Kurt gave her a shy smile, "I didn't start this. It's all Faelynn's fault. She finds out all this stuff and drags me along with her for my opinion. You should see what a hard cookie she is when it comes to dealing with people. It would make your knees quake." He shouted, "Ouch." and rubbed his leg under the table and gave her a hard stare before finishing, "Well, you are."

Then they all laughed. Faelynn corrected Kurt's statement, "I didn't have the orphanage experience but I had my own hardships. I wanted to make sure that the sleazy Reverend didn't take the money we gave him to benefit himself. I meant it to be spent on those babies. We've set up a board to oversea the home and make sure the books are on the up and up and that the kids have decent food and beds to sleep in at night. I think that is both Kurt and my idea. As Kurt said, we want them to be able to laugh now and then without having to worry about surviving day to day." Richard reached over and squeezed her hand and Diane did the same. Richard turned to Kurt, "I'm glad to know I had misjudged you terribly and want you to know how sorry I am that I jumped to that conclusion. I'm going to be very proud to have you as my brother-in-law."

He reached across the table and shook hands with Kurt; they even smiled at each other. Kurt smiled at his new sister and spoke kindly, "Since knowing Faelynn as family it seems my charitable side is showing a lot more. She made it possible for me to dream of the things we could do together to help the ones that were left behind. The four of us will be close and I want you all to know I'm so pleased to be included in this family." Diane concurred, "Amen, me too." Richard, not to be out done said, "Amen, me three." They shared another laugh before finishing their meal and getting back into the car. Kurt asked all of them, "Would you like to drive by the orphanage to see the changes?" All of them agreed so when they found Janie Walker they would swing by there for a surprise visit.

They drove to the address that they had for Janie Walker and sat in the car watching the apartment. They talked of several things while waiting to catch a glimpse of their subject. Faelynn turned to Diane, "Have you and Kurt set a date to get married yet?" Diane shook her head no, "We were just wondering if you and Richard had set a date yet too." Richard popped in with a solution, "I hope it's soon I'm getting tired of sleeping alone. I think I've waited long enough; we can go to a JP and get married tomorrow. Hey wait a minute; I can marry us all right here and now." Faelynn looked at him like he had lost his mind. "What! You expect me to believe you and marry us without a license?" He smiled slyly and whispered, "Well, I could." Kurt looked at Diane, "Want to get married right now in this car?" She laughed and pushed his arm, "I think not. I'd at least like to have a small wedding, nothing elaborate or fancy just family and a few friends." He kissed her on the cheek, "You deserve that and more my love."

Richard looked at Kurt and frowned, "I was getting it all set up so we could spend the night with them. Why did you go and spoil it?" They all chuckled because they knew he was just kidding. Soon they saw the door to the apartment they were watching open and a woman with four kids came out. She walked them down the stairs and out to a little swing set near the apartment complex. She stayed right with the kids as she watched them play. She talked to a few other ladies from the apartments that were they're doing the same thing.

The foursome watched her for a long time then gave their assessment of what they thought of her. Kurt gave his first, "She does seem to be a good mother. I like that. Wonder what happened to her husband. Perhaps death or divorce but he must not be paying child support." The next one to speak was Diane; "I too, like the fact that she is staying right with the kids. In this neighborhood I'd be careful too. She seems neat and the kids are clean." Richard agreed with them both, "Yes, she is a clean person and a good mother." Faelynn weighted in with her view. "I think we all agree she is a good mother but we need to know where the father is and what the deal is with child support. That apartment rent has to be either low income or subsidized. We should call the attorney and see if he has that information or can he get it."

They drove away headed toward the orphanage. They pulled into the street where the orphanage was and all sat in the car staring at the place. Kurt told them of what it had been like, "When we were here before the house was unpainted, a dirt yard and hardly any windows, they were boarded up. Three ladies were taking care of about fifteen children and there were no beds, they had to sleep on the floor on mattresses. They were in filthy clothes and un-bathed." Faelynn told the rest of the story, "The Reverend, a shyster of sorts, had beautiful antiques and velvet furniture in his office and home. I think all the donations that came here went to his pocket. That is why

Kurt and I insisted an audit be done every six months to keep him straight. Lucky for us he chose to resign rather than report all the donations. Now, there is a new group in place and it looks like they are cleaning it up nicely."

They all looked at the nice white building with a large play yard with swings, slides and cars to ride in. There was a high fence around the place so the kids didn't wonder into the street. There had been a small house built between the orphanage and the office. Faelynn wondered why they had done that instead of utilizing the upper rooms of the office area. "Why would they build another office with a whole floor above the office?"

Kurt jumped out of the car and danced around it a few times. Faelynn got out and looked at him as if he had gone daffy. She yelled at him, "What is it you are thinking?" He stopped and got his breath while the other two got out of the car. He raised his hands in the air dancing, "I've got it; I've got the answer to our prayers." Now, he was being stared at by three sets of eyes with questions too. He laughed and grabbed Diane and squeezed her to him. Faelynn stamped her foot about ready to choke him for not sharing his idea, "Okay brother; spit it out now!" He couldn't stop laughing then Richard crossed his arms over his chest, "I think I'll withdraw my past opinion of Kurt." He then smiled and put his arm around Faelynn and pulled her to him. Kurt stopped and calmed down catching his breath, "I have the perfect solution to our dilemma. We need a new job for Janie Walker right?" They all agreed he was right. "Well, this is the perfect place to put her. She can be the onsite social worker for the children. It's only obvious she loves children and she works for the government as a social worker. Now, this is the best part. We subsidized her earnings as long as she goes to school to get her degree in social studies and then her Master's degree. Once she has the degree then she can get a better job. Perhaps, if she wants to stay here we can make her the overseer of this operation. She would have her own home no expense for getting to the job; her kids would be perfectly safe. What a great idea? What do you all think?"

They looked at him with an astonished look. He was right this would be perfect for her. She could make sure the kids were taken care of and she would have a safe place for her kids too. Faelynn grabbed him and hugged him yelling with him now. "Yes, it's perfect. Let's get back to town and call the attorney to have him set it up. Good thinking Kurt." Diane looked at Richard and asked, "Do you think we're going to be safe with them around?" She then laughed and hugged Kurt and kissed him soundly. "That's for being a great person." He held onto her and asked for more. So she kissed him again. Richard held Faelynn close to him and whispered, "Let's get back in the car before the police come and arrest us for acting crazy." But once in the car he pulled her into his arms and kissed her again.

Kurt and Diane got into the car and they headed back to Covington. They talked all the way about how they could help to get her to the orphanage. Faelynn was so pleased with the whole idea, "Now that we have that issue settled. What about our marriage plans? Do we want to do this together or have separate weddings? Diane, how do you feel about this?" Diane laugh, "Faelynn, I don't care if we get married in our pajamas as long as Kurt and I are both there at the same time." Kurt turned to Diane, "Would you object to a double wedding Diane?" She shook her head, "No, I did mean that, as long as we're there together, I'd follow you to the end of the earth to marry you." He drew her into his arms and gave her a very passionate kiss.

Faelynn looked at Richard, "Would you object to a double wedding Richard?" He shook his head, "No, I'm with Diane, as long as you're saying yes to me then I'm a happy camper." Faelynn looked at Kurt, "Kurt, what do you think?" He patted his sister's shoulder, "I think it would be the coolest thing we ever do. If you're game so am I. Just think years down the road we could go out to dinner together hobbling along with our walkers celebrating our fiftieth anniversary." They all laughed.

They arrived back in Covington and stopped at the hospital for Kurt and Diane to get their car. Faelynn got out and hugged them both, "Thank you so much for such a great evening and we'll do it again soon. Talk to you both later." She saw them pulling out shortly after they had entered the street. She slid over close to Richard and laid her head on his shoulder. He rubbed his cheek on her head, "Did you have a nice time with them?" She smiled and thought of the fun the four of them had. They would have had fun growing up together, "Yes, it was fun wasn't it. I've never had anyone around me so energetic." Then she laughed, "Did you enjoy it or was it too much for you." He had stopped at a red light and leaned close enough for a quick kiss. "I loved every minute of it especially right now when we're alone and I know you love me. Can we plan the wedding quickly so we can live together?" She grinned at him, "Yes very soon."

He pulled into her yard and cut off the car. "I think we should sit here for an hour or so just kissing and hugging." She slid into his embrace and moaned when his kiss ended. "Yes, we need to plan the wedding very soon." He opened the door and helped her out and they went into the house. It was dark so she cut on a few lights. He kissed her good night and he stepped outside her door and walked to his car. She locked the door and cut on the outside light. She walked up the stairs and went to bed.

EPILOGUE

Faelynn and Kurt had a double wedding. Both couples were beautiful and the church was filled with flowers. The ceremony was a small one with just a few friends and family present. Phyllis and Annie were there from Oregon, a gift from Richard to Faelynn. They were put at the best hotel in Atlanta for a one-week stay, along with a lot of brochures of places to see and things to do. Faelynn made sure a limo was at their disposal in case they wanted to go anywhere.

Kurt and Faelynn talked to grandmother about having someone stay with her while they were away. She quickly replied that Randall Morrison could stay with her. Faelynn and Kurt raised their eyebrows and their grandmother told them in her reprimanding voice, "I'm well over the age of consent so get your minds out of the gutter." They all hugged and laughed a lot before their plane left for Hawaii.

Randall had moved into the guest room which Kurt and Diane had vacated just a few days before. They were now encased into their family home. Richard and Faelynn were building a large home on grandmother's additional land that they had owned for many years. Their new home would have at least six to eight bedrooms with baths. They seemed to be planning on a large family with a few adoptions thrown in for good measure. Alexandria was staying with Richard's mother until their return. Richard's mom was taking her on a sightseeing tour to Florida and would end up at Disneyland or Sea World before returning to Georgia.

Kurt and Faelynn decided to build a wing onto the hospital with their charity fund for children with special injuries and fatal or terminal diseases. They could get specialized treatment there. It would be one of the finest children's wings in the whole state with the best doctors manning it. Kurt's name change went through and now he was Dr. Myers. So the family home was transferred to him also.

They kept tabs on the orphanage in Alabama where they both were adopted. It seems that Janie Walker had accepted the position offered to her and she was now living on the grounds of the orphanage and going back to school. The board that was overseeing the orphanage had it cleaned up nicely and was making sure that the kids would be cared for first not last. They had medical care, nourishing food, beds to sleep in and clean clothes to wear and regular baths.

Oh, and the money they left in the stock market had already built back up to where it was when they divided it out. So they divided it the same as last time and that will give them more money for their favorite charities. Both Kurt and Faelynn knew their father was a financial genius.

When they returned they would follow up with the detective to see if he had gotten Ramona Smith from Austin, Texas to take the fifty thousand dollars in a claimed insurance policy from his job. A recheck of Lois Moon's situation saw a marriage announcement in the paper for her and her friend at the company, so she was going to be fine. A few years ago there was a grandmother and her granddaughter and today their family was growing by leaps and bounds. The very best part of this was finally, there was a close family bond where once there was nothing. Life is good sprinkled with family and love, yes, lots of love.

THE END

Would you like to see your manuscript become a book?

If you are interested in becoming a PublishAmerica author, please submit your manuscript for possible publication to us at:

acquisitions@publishamerica.com

You may also mail in your manuscript to:

**PublishAmerica
PO Box 151
Frederick, MD 21705**

We also offer free graphics for Children's Picture Books!

www.publishamerica.com